The Light That Was Lucia

Moving Beyond Secrecy and Shame

Felice Falzarano

Contents

Foreword

From A Friend

Some stories arrive not with fanfare, but like soft light at dawn, silently, searching, and unforgettable. *"The Light That Was Lucia"* is one of those stories.

Set in the sun-warmed hills of southern Italy, this is not merely a tale of first love or youthful discovery. It is a memory wrapped in time, a reflection of what it means to feel deeply, to hope boldly, and to lose gently.

In these pages, Felice offers us more than a recollection of a chapter from his youth, he gives us a window into a world where faith and longing lived side by side, and where a single encounter could alter the course of a heart forever.

His story, like the girl he remembers, is luminous. To read this book is to walk with Felice through quiet seminars, convents, bustling Benevento streets, and the secret corners of the heart.

It is to see a light that once was—and still is, in memory, in words, and in love that never fully fades.

Giovanni Perrotta, Paolisi

Author's Voice

There are moments in life that never quite leave us. They remain, not as chapters fully closed, but as breath held between memory and dream.

"The Light That Was Lucia" is born from such a moment. This is not a tale of romance in the conventional sense. It is a quiet story, drawn from a time and place where youth walked hand in hand with faith, and where a glance could carry more weight than words.

Lucia was not simply a girl I once knew. She was the light that revealed something within me—about love, about hope, and about the quiet ache of letting go. This book is my attempt to honor her, not only as she was then, but as she remains, glowing in the edge of memory.

If you have once loved in silence, or remembered someone more clearly than you understand them, then this story is for you.

Thank You. *Felice Falzarano*

Palm Beach Gardens, Florida. May 2025

Introduction

Every one of us has secrets. Some we barely understand ourselves. Others, we try to hide so badly, afraid of ruining the image we've built, the version of ourselves we want others to see.

However, keeping secrets doesn't protect us the way we think it does. It builds walls, thinking at first that we're shielding ourselves, or the people we care about.

But over time, those secrets keep us from getting closer to others. And when that happens, we begin to lie; to others and ourselves.

So, I say that everyone has secrets. Some could be small and harmless, things that fade with time. Others never do; they linger in the shadows of our memory, shaping us, quietly influencing the way we move through the world.

I have to confess: I have a few of those.

For more than six decades, I carried these stories inside me that I never shared with anyone. Not because I was ashamed of it, but because I didn't know how to share them, how to put into words something beautiful or painful, and completely unexpected all at once.

Keeping secrets, I've learned, doesn't just distance us from others; it creates a kind of dishonesty with ourselves. We protect an image, a version of who we think we should be, even when it's not the whole truth.

Some of the secrets we carry are small, almost harmless, while others are heavy, life-shaping truths we keep buried for years, because we don't know what will happen if we speak about them.

With this memoir, I'm making an attempt to change that. To finally tell the truth, because I've carried more than one secret.

The main story I'm about to share is one I've held close for six decades. It's a story about a love I wasn't supposed to have, and a truth I never saw coming.

But that's not the only secret I've kept. The earlier ones started from the moment I began to understand.

It all began in a small town where I was born and raised. My earliest memories go back to when I was just six years old, when I started to learn about my father.

My story continues when I was sixteen, living in a seminary, preparing, at least on paper, for the priesthood.

My father, may he rest in peace, had a temper. He was verbally abusive towards my mother, loud and cruel when things didn't go his way.

He was also a womanizer. I saw him with my own eyes, saw him cheat, saw the lies, the excuses, and the quiet pain it brought into our home. We all saw it. We just didn't speak about it.

He had a few obsessions: one, that one of us boys, my brother and I, would become a priest, as if that would redeem something in him.

The other was emigration. It chased it like it held the answer to a better life. He dragged us through three different migrations, thinking that it would have changed our future that never quite arrived, at least not from the first two occasions.

So, that was the world I grew up in, a little chaotic, uncertain, built on silence and forced paths.

This book is, more than anything, about a girl that I met when I was just sixteen. At the beginning, it was something new, and it felt like something real.

It happened at a moment when we were both supposed to become something else, me a priest, she a nun, but neither of us truly belonged to those futures.

What happened between us wasn't just love; there was something deeper, and what I discovered later shook the foundation of everything I believed about myself and my family, especially about my father.

I'm telling this story now because silence, in the end, costs more than truth; it separates us from others, and eventually, from who we really are.

This is my truth, finally spoken.

Chapter 1

Years ago, during a school lesson, I came across a quote that stayed with me. It was from Mark Twain.

He wrote, *"The two most important days of your life are the day you're born and the day you find out why."*

At the time, I didn't fully understand what it meant, but the words sank into me regardless, and they never left. Over the years, I kept coming back to them, especially during moments of doubt and silence.

I asked myself many times: *"Why was I born? Was there a reason? A purpose? A meaning?*

Life has a way of unfolding slowly, sometimes painfully. We search for meaning in what happens to us, in the places we're taken, in the people we meet, in the things we lose.

I didn't know it then, but looking back now, I believe that love, no matter how complicated or unexpected, is part of that answer.

Yes, the story is about love. But it's also about discovery, identity, family, silence, and truth. And it's about how the answer to why we're here may not come all at once, but through the lives we touch and through the courage we find to face the things we never meant to carry.

I thought about that phrase for years. It didn't matter how many times I read or how long I waited for an answer; nothing that made sense ever came to my mind.

Not finding a sensible answer led me to the conclusion that maybe I wasn't born for anything. Maybe I just… was. I told myself, *"You just happened to be born."* For no grand purpose, or for no chosen path, but just for a life set in motion by the choice of others.

That thought stayed with me for years. Not in a bitter way, but in a quiet, unsettled way. It shaped how I saw myself, how I let life happen to me, instead of asking what I really wanted.

But life doesn't always ask our permission for what happens. Sometimes, in the middle of the drafting, something, or someone, comes along that changes everything.

And when one's life takes a certain turn, suddenly, you're no longer just existing. You're awake.

That's what this story is all about. It's about the moment I woke up, when many times I found myself staring at the ceiling, quietly asking the famous question: *"Why was I born?"*

As a good Catholic and a devoted altar boy, I believed, truly believed, that God had created me for a reason. That my life wasn't an accident or a coincidence, but part of something greater.

He had given me a purpose, even if I couldn't see it clearly; that purpose, I felt, was tied to the essence of who I was, my true self.

It gave me the quiet reassurance that I mattered. Not just to Him, but to the people in my life. Somehow, I was meant to bring something good into the world, even if I yet knew what it was.

Sometimes, that belief was the only thing that kept me going, even in the seminary where life wasn't easy. The days were long, the rules strict, the silence often overwhelming. But I held on to the idea that my being there was of God's plan, even if the path wasn't clear yet.

There were moments when doubt crept in, quiet and persistent. I'd watch other boys, some confident, some lost, and wondered if they too asked the same question in the dark.

Maybe we all carry our private conversations with God, hoping for answers, signs, or at least some peace. But faith, as I was learning, wasn't always about answers.

Sometimes, it was about learning to live inside the question, trusting that the purpose would reveal itself in time.

And perhaps it did, one morning, in a theater seat I hadn't planned to take, when a girl I wasn't supposed to meet looked over and smiled.

Now I want to be clear about something: I'm not ashamed of what I'm about to write in this book. This story, my story, isn't just about memories or confession; it's about breaking a damaging cycle of secrets.

Secrets create walls between people; they lead to dishonesty, silence, and pain passed down from one generation to the next.

What I'm ashamed of, what still tightens in my chest when I think about it, is the crushing moment when I learned the truth about the girl I started dating.

She was the one who, for the first time, had stirred something new, confusing, and beautiful in me, but eventually I realized that she was my half-sister.

Even now, it's hard to write those words. I was so young, so full of questions, of longing, of hope. We had grown close, closer than we should have, and though we hadn't gone all the way, we had come very close.

When the truth came out, it wasn't just disappointment I felt. It was deflation. Like the very air had been pulled out of me. I felt the world shifting under my feet, and I didn't know who I was anymore.

I know people will judge me for telling this, maybe even for living it. Sharing something so private feels like peeling back skin, exposing what was never meant to be seen. And I understand. People judge. It's human nature.

But what I don't know, what I doubt, is whether they truly understand the circumstances. The isolation. The silence. The way secrets were kept, not out of malice, but out of fear and shame.

I didn't grow up with the whole truth. I wasn't given the map, but only fragments of it. So when I made mistakes, when I stumbled into something that should never have happened, it wasn't out of rebellion or carelessness.

It was out of longing for love, connection, and something that felt like it had been missing my entire life.

The fact that I'm not shaming myself anymore makes it easier to write about it. There's freedom in facing the truth without turning it into a weapon against myself.

For too long, I have carried the weight of that experience like it defined me. Like it disqualified me from love, from belonging, from grace. But I have learned that shame deepens the wound.

That doesn't mean it's easy. Revisiting these painful, traumatic events still takes something out of me. It stirs emotions I've spent years trying to quiet: grief, confusion, and even guilt.

Writing about them feels like walking through the fire again, knowing it might burn, but hoping it will also cleanse.

Still, I believe this is the only way forward. If I don't speak, if I don't remember honestly, then I stay stuck in a past I never chose. And I can't let that happen. Not anymore.

Some people say that writing autobiographies is inherently subjective, that memory is unreliable, that we shape the past to fit the story we want to tell.

Maybe that's true for some. But for me, there's no need to wrestle with questions of accuracy or hidden bias. I'm not here to embellish or edit my truth. I'm here to face it.

I despise writing an autobiography. I don't enjoy it. It doesn't bring me peace or pleasure. If anything, it drags me through the mud of my past, forcing me to confront things I'd rather forget. And yet I write.

Because in spite of the pain, this story matters. It offers a window, unfiltered, unadorned, into a life shaped by love won and lost, by mistakes made and wisdom earned the hard way. If even one person finds truth in these pages, then maybe the discomfort is worth it.

The words I'm about to write are pieces of myself. Memories carved into my skin, thoughts I've carried in silence for far too long.

And I know that, at some point, I'll want to swallow them back. Because these words will hurt. They already do.

But I'm going on with it anyway.

I understand that people will judge me. They'll judge the choice I made, the feelings I had, and the people involved, some of whom never asked to be part of this story. And I refuse to stay silent anymore.

So I invite you, whoever you are, to stay with me. To read this story not with the finger ready to point, but with a heart willing to listen.

Chapter 2

I was born in a typical small town in the province of Benevento, Italy. Like many other families in the region, mine was deeply rooted in Catholic tradition. Religion wasn't just a belief; it was a way of life.

I grew up attending Sunday Mass regularly. As an altar boy, I served at the altar with pride and devotion, my small hands learned the rituals passed down through generations.

I also took part in meetings of the Catholic association, where we gathered for prayers, community, and shaping young minds into faithful men.

As I grew older, though, I began to notice things, disgusting, heartbreaking things, that didn't seem to belong in the world I was told to believe in.

I saw young children born with incurable diseases, families shattered by loss, and I began to question the very faith I was raised with.

Weren't things supposed to be different if God was real? I couldn't understand how a loving God would allow parents to bury their children.

That thought hunted me. It clashed with the comforting, orderly vision of faith I had grown up with, and I started to inquire, quietly, if God truly existed.

But in a family like mine, where Catholicism was more than belief, it was heritage; those questions had little room to breathe. The strong cultural force of religion overshadowed my doubts, pressed them down like weeds beneath a stone.

It wasn't until much later in my life that I realized that Catholicism, for me, had been more of a legacy than a living belief. Something passed down like an heirloom, rather than something I had chosen freely.

Still, I remained a good Catholic boy. As a teenager, I continued to serve as an altar boy, and I believed in the power of confession. I regularly sat with the archpriest, listing my sins, and seeking absolution.

But even in the confessional, I wasn't always honest. At times, I sinned twice, once in my actions and again in my silence. Many times I held back the truth, afraid of what it would mean to speak it aloud.

The worst secret I ever kept wasn't just from the priest; it was from my own mother. How could I tell her what I had seen?

Later in his story, I'll explain how and when I saw my father, with my own eyes, with another woman. It wasn't a rumor or a suspicion. It was real, and I had buried it inside me like a stone.

I carried it in silence, afraid that it would destroy her, afraid it would destroy us. But that silence came at a cost. It ate away at me, made me feel like I was part of the betrayal just by knowing.

I often wondered if telling would have made any difference at all. A part of me believed it wouldn't. She loved him, maybe blindly, maybe out of duty, and in those days, no one talked about divorce.

It was unthinkable, especially in a Catholic household. A woman was expected to endure, to forgive, to keep the family together at all costs.

But the affair wasn't my father's only betrayal. His jealousy turned into something darker, an abusive, controlling anger that he directed at my mother. He belittled her, broke her down, and made her small in her own home.

And she took it quietly. She never raised her voice, never fought back, never tried to leave. Maybe she thought she couldn't.

Maybe she believed that suffering in silence was her cross to bear. Or maybe she had simply grown numb to it all.

Watching it unfold, I felt helpless, angry, but most of all confused. And that confusion stayed with me, shaping how I understood love, trust, and the complicated silence that often fills a home.

My father had other obsessions too. When I was just six years old, he began talking endlessly about immigration. At first it was Argentina, then it was Australia, and then finally the USA.

He spoke of these places like a promised land, far from the struggle of our small town. He carried dreams of escape, of building a better life, though I don't think he ever really knew what that meant for the rest of us.

Later, when I became a teenager, his obsession shifted. This time, it was the priesthood. He became fixated on the idea that one of his sons would become a priest.

It wasn't a gentle hope or a quiet prayer. It was an expectation, a pressure that settled heavily on my shoulders, being that I was the oldest.

Maybe he thought it would bring honor to the family. Maybe he believed it would redeem something broken in himself. Or maybe, deep down, he wanted to control what he couldn't fix in his own soul.

I can't say for sure. But I know that his dreams, like his temper, had a way of taking up all the space in the room.

Most of the time, I loved my father, though many times, I hated him, or at least, I felt like I did. There were moments, especially when I watched him treat my mother so cruelly, that I imagined hurting him, killing him, so to speak. That's how much the anger burned in me.

The idea of forgiving him felt absurd. How do you forgive someone who hurt the person you love most? The one who made your home feel like a place of quiet fear instead of safety?

And yet…I miss him. He's been gone for many years now, and not a day passes without a memory sneaking in, mostly tender, some bitter.

I remember the long walks we used to take on Sundays on the rural road that led us to his parents' farm. Just the two of us, his pace slow, his stories flowing.

I remember how he taught me to drive, patient and focused, never raising his voice, never losing his temper with us, his children.

As a truck driver, he worked hard, long, grueling hours to provide for the family. We never went without the essentials. In his way, he did care for his family.

He loved us, but I know that he loved my mother more than anything in the world, even if he didn't always know how to show it in the right way.

This narrative, at its core, is my way of coming clean about the life I lived, the choice I made, and the things I've carried for too long.

There were moments, I'll admit, when I thought about changing the storyline. Perhaps softening it a little. Hiding behind the excuse of memory or shaping the facts to be more palatable. But that would go against everything I've set out to do.

From the beginning, my intention has been clear: *No more secrets. Move beyond secrecy and shame.* And if I'm serious about that, then I can't just expose my father's failures and pretend my hands are clean. I have to open the door of my own dark corners, too.

Because I'm not a saint. I never was. I've made mistakes, some small, some impossible to forget. But if I want to speak with honesty, I have to speak fully, even if it means standing naked in front of the truth.

Confiding secrets, besides being purifying and liberating, can reduce the emotional weight we carry. There's something powerful about finally giving shape to what we've kept hidden. Putting it into words. Releasing it from the shadow of the mind.

But then comes the question: *To whom can you tell these secrets?*

It's not as simple as it sounds. Finding someone who is truly open-minded, reliable, scrupulous, and trustworthy is easier said than done.

Some people listen only to judge. Others betray what was never theirs to share. So most of us stay silent, not because we want to, but because we're afraid.

For years, I have been running away from the truth. I carried it like a burden strapped on my back, heavy and imprisoning. But the weight became too much. I realized that secrecy was not protecting me; it was breaking me.

That's why I've chosen to embrace transparency and reality. To speak plainly, even when it hurts. To write not just for others, but for myself. This is my cleansing, my reckoning, and my release.

Chapter 3

My life has been a long journey, one marked by time, fewer choices, detours, and moments I never saw coming.

Like anyone, I began with dreams and ideals, but the path ahead rarely matched the one I thought I was following.

There were times I felt completely lost, unsure of who I was or where I was going, and more than once, I doubted I'd ever find my way back. And yet, somehow, I always did.

Whether by grace, by stubbornness, or by the quiet strength I didn't know I had, I kept going. I rebuilt myself, piece by piece, memory by memory.

Much later in life, when I thought certain chapters had already closed, I met the woman who changed everything. She didn't fix me; she simply made the pieces I'd gathered along the way fit together in a way that finally made sense.

With her, I saw the full picture, and it was more beautiful than I had ever imagined.

I was born into a middle-class family in southern Italy. My father was a truck driver, a man of hard work and few words. My mother was a simple housewife, gentle, devoted, and quietly strong in her way.

Life was modest but steady, rooted in traditions, family, and faith. When I was still young, about five/six years old, my father made bold decisions that would shape my life in ways I couldn't yet understand.

Like many Italians in the years after the war, he was chasing something better, opportunity perhaps, or simply a new beginning. Maybe he was also running from something. I was too young to know.

The places where he wanted us children to find a better future were a world away from the quiet town where I was born.

I was still just a little boy when the first move started, too young to understand why we left or what we were supposed to find there.

I only remember the strangeness of it all, the sound of a new language, the different smell in the streets, the brightness of the sun that felt hotter than anything I'd known back home.

At first, everything felt like an adventure. But even in my childish mind, I could sense the undercurrent of struggle. My parents worked hard to adapt, especially my mother.

My father found work; he always did, but it wasn't what he had imagined. My mother missed her home, her family, her language. And we all realized that life in those strange lands was not the dream my father had sold us.

We lived there long enough for me to start understanding a new language, to start making small friendships in the neighborhood and in school.

I was just a little boy, but no matter where I went, I was able to enroll in a strange school. There was something that always felt temporary, as if we were just visitors passing through.

Eventually, my father would have a change of heart, a decision that would take us back to Italy and return me to the path that would define much of my youth.

That story, the moment, the date, and how it all started, I will share it soon. Because what happened during those months, and what led my father to turn around, matters deeply. It left marks that stayed with me, even when the memories faded.

So I was six years old when my father started to talk about us emigrating, but he never mentioned a precise destination.

I was listening to those conversations, especially on Sunday mornings when my father was usually home from work, and sat in the kitchen with my mother to have breakfast together.

Since my bedroom was only steps away, usually, I would be woken up by their conversation, and I carefully listened to every word they said.

On one such morning I was there having breakfast with the two of them. It was the first time I heard my father mentioning Buenos Aires, Argentina.

They spoke quietly, but I was old enough to understand what was about to take place.

My mother shrugged her shoulders and said, "Why emigrate, Domenico? What is the reason?"

My father ran his hand through his hair, his gaze fixed somewhere far away, and replied, "Antonietta, for the children. For a better future."

"Domenico, if you want to give the children a better future, why aren't we going to the USA. It would be easier, since I'm an American citizen."

But my father never listened to my mother, and that was the moment everything shifted. The decision had already been made, and we were scheduled to leave on August 16th, 1955.

I was a month away from turning seven, and I remember that day vividly. The moment we climbed into the van that would take us to the ship, I felt something in me break, an invisible thread to the home I was already beginning to miss.

When we arrived at the port and I saw the name of the ship written on the bow, I began to cry.

The name was Nostalgia. How appropriate that was. Nostalgia had already wrapped itself around my whole body and soul before we even boarded.

I didn't have the words for it then, but I knew I was leaving behind more than just a place. I was leaving a piece of myself.

My mother was a U.S. citizen by birth. She was born in New York, but her parents had returned to Italy when she was just six years old.

So, when my father brought up the idea of emigrating, she had a different destination in her mind.

"If I want to go someplace," she asked him many times, "Why not the United States?"

It was a fair question. America wasn't a stranger to her, at least not entirely. She had the necessary paperwork, the connection by blood, and perhaps some faint memories of a different kind of life.

But my father shook his head. "I have a cousin in Argentina," he said. "We have no one in the United States."

That was it. That one thread of familiarity, one cousin in a foreign land, was enough to tip the scale.

Logic, paperwork, and even citizenship took a back seat to the comfort of knowing someone would be there.

Looking back, I sometimes wonder how different our lives would've been if we had boarded a ship headed west across the Atlantic instead of south across it.

But that was the choice, and once it was made, there was no turning back. As fate would have it, many years later, we did come to the United States.

But that's a different chapter in the story, one that came after much wondering, after lessons learned and paths crossed that we could have never imagined back then.

At that time, Argentina was our chosen destination. And it was there, in that faraway country, that a new chapter of my childhood began.

I knew how to read somehow, and under my mother's guidance, I always took notes in my sloppy diary.

Yes, even if I was just seven, I had a diary. It was my first diary, full of good and bad memories. I kept it for all the years, like a treasure, with all the others. That is where all this information is coming from.

The day of the departure was sunny and hot, and when we got to the port in Naples. Once we embarked, the first thing we did, like everyone else, was to go up on deck and wave goodbye to our relatives and friends.

While up there, I watched the mooring lines that secured the vessel to the berth being released, and the ship slowly moved away from the dock to navigate out of the port.

I watched my mother in tears, weaving a white handkerchief, saying goodbye to her sad parents, who were becoming smaller and smaller, until they disappeared from my sight.

I remember that the first day spent at sea was on a sunny Monday, and the Mediterranean Sea was calm, and the weather was fine during the night.

I believe it was on Wednesday morning when we had a clear view of the Gibraltar Strait. As we were crossing it, my father reminded me that we were about to leave the Mediterranean Sea, and would soon cross over to the Atlantic Ocean.

During the first part of the day the wind was light, but as we were eating lunch in the restaurant, the ship started racking. That scared me, and I became all worried.

Late that night, we got hit by a violent storm. Rain was beating up on the ship, and the wind was hauling. It was my first time on a huge boat in the middle of the ocean, and I was scared, but my parents kept on telling me not to worry so much.

By the morning, the storm was gone, the sky was clear of the clouds, and the wind became fairer. It became more pleasant halfway through the first part of the day, but in the evening the weather changed again, and we had the same experience as the previous night.

As a child, I was always observant and very curious. I wanted to know how many more days I would have to be on that ship before I could meet new friends. Perhaps play soccer with them, since for Argentina it's a national sport, as it is in my country.

One day, while we were outside taking in some fresh air, I asked the first person I saw there working on the boat. "Signore, how long does it take to get to Buenos Aires?"

"About 16 days altogether, little boy. So, from today another twelve," he said.

"Another twelve days of the same boring routine?" I asked. "Why so long?"

The sailor smiled at me. "America is far, little man. Besides, we're not going straight to Buenos Aires. The ship will make two other stops before getting there."

Just like the man said, the ship navigated for two long, interminable weeks. As expected, it made the first stop in Rio de Janeiro, then the second one in Montevideo, and then, finally, days later, we reached Buenos Aires.

At every one of those stops, immigrants awaited by friends and relatives were getting off the ship, but during that process, we were not allowed to do the same.

After two weeks on that ship, we finally reached our final destination: "Buenos Aires." A cousin of my father was there to greet us as we disembarked.

We settled in a small town called Paso del Rey, just outside Buenos Aires. It was a quiet place, far from the noise and energy of the city, with dusty roads and rows of modest houses.

For a little boy like me, it felt foreign and wide open at the same time, a place where everything looked similar but felt different.

Our home was simple. The walls were thin, the floors creaked, and the air smelled different, like sunbaked earth and cooking oil.

One thing I remember clearly, no need to consult my diary: it rained a lot in that part of the country! Every time it did, we would experience power outages for hours.

I knew my mother was not so happy to be there, but since she was a tolerant woman, we never once heard her complain about it. She did her best to make it feel warm and familiar, but I could see in her eyes that she was homesick.

My father found work quickly; he always did. He was dependable, hardworking, and willing to do whatever it took to support us.

But I don't think his heart was ever really in it. He carried himself with a quiet tension, like a man trying to convince himself that he hadn't made a mistake.

I was enrolled in school, where the language barrier made me feel lost. I didn't speak Spanish, and my accent set me apart.

I was the strange boy in the classroom–awkward, silent, my Italian words curling up in my mouth before they could escape.

Everything felt upside down. The sun was too hot, the seasons were backwards, the kids had a rhythm I couldn't follow.

I remember the dust in the schoolyard, the sing-song Spanish that echoed around me, the teachers who didn't quite know what to do with me.

I must have looked lost–because I was. I didn't understand the jokes, the games, the way things worked.

On weekends, I noticed the men in the neighborhood drinking out in the street, openly, carelessly. They were sometimes loud, sometimes laughing, and sometimes angry.

It confused me. Back home in Italy, people drank too, but here it felt different–less measured, more like escape.

I don't even remember anymore what I was thinking in those early days. I was too young to name the sadness, too small to understand the size of the world I had just been thrown into.

All I knew was that I didn't belong there. But somehow, life went on. Still, I remember the kindness of a few kids who helped me find my way, small gestures that meant the world to a frightened boy in a strange land.

Paso del Rey was meant to be the beginning. But in many ways, it felt more like a pause, a moment between one life and the next.

Christmas came, then the New Year. For us, as a family, it was boring, it was the first Holiday without our traditional Christmas-eve dinner with my grandparents and other family members.

We hardly knew anyone there. Even if most people spoke Italian, we didn't have enough time to make real friends. In just six months, my father came to a decision that surprised even him.

Six months. That's all it took.

Whatever dream my father brought with him to Argentina began to fade almost as soon as we arrived. The work was hard, the cost of living was higher than expected, and the cousin he had relied on for support had problems of his own.

My mother missed Italy terribly. Her homesickness was like a second presence in the house, quiet but heavy. I think, deep down, my father realized he had dragged us across the world chasing something that didn't really exist.

He didn't talk much about his decision. That wasn't his way. Although I truly believe that someone up there must have heard my prayers. Because not long after, something changed in my father's head.

Maybe it was the weight of being far from home, maybe it was the struggle of making a life in a country that never felt like ours. Or maybe, just maybe, he was enlightened by something greater.

One evening, while having dinner, I overheard him say to my mother, "Antonietta, we're going back. This isn't the life I wanted for you, and especially for the kids."

My mother sighed. "Yes, Domenico, I've been telling you that this place is not for us. Let's go back. At least we have our own house there."

He nodded. "Antonietta, we gave it a try. I'm sorry it didn't work out. We have the money for the trip. I'll get my job back as soon as we get home, so no worry, we'll soon be back home."

So just as suddenly as we had left, we packed up once more. I didn't understand all the reasons, but I didn't question them either. As a seven-year-old, who believed in God, I only knew that my silent wish to go back to the land where my voice had once made sense had been answered.

On the return trip, we boarded the same ship, Nostalgia.

I remember standing on the dock and seeing her name again, just as I had six months earlier. But this time, my tears were different.

They were not tears of sadness, but of relief.

We were going home. I didn't fully understand what that meant at that time, but I knew enough to feel the weight of it lift off my small shoulders.

My father never spoke of Argentina again, not with regret, and certainly not with pride. It became one of those things families silently agree to fold away in memory, like a photo you keep safe but never in a frame.

It was on a February day of 1956 when we left Buenos Aires, and in a little more than two weeks, we reached the port of Naples, where my grandparents were waiting for us.

I was able to enroll in the second year of elementary school. My friends were so happy to see me back. Most of all, I was happy to be back; at the same time, I hoped that my father wouldn't get any new ideas about going to strange places.

I didn't know, but to tell the truth, I didn't care about exactly why my father didn't want to stay in Argentina. Maybe it was the lack of adaptation, like he was saying, or even nostalgia.

I was too little to want to know, or to even understand why, back then, but years later, as an adolescent, I learned that despite the well-known integration of migrants in the Argentine life, failure to adapt to local life, or nostalgia were the main cause of attempts to return, and for many people, to return permanently, just like we did.

Perhaps, even in the attempts to return, there is the effect of the eradication and the weight of nostalgia. At least, that was what I learned when talking to my parents and some other people who had had the same experience back then.

Those two things didn't have an effect on me at all. I was happy to be back in my native land. Back in my environment, back to school with my friends, and most importantly, with my grandparents.

A few years passed, and before I could realize it, I was thirteen. As a teenager, it seemed to me that my life changed daily, being constantly exposed to new ideas, social situations, and people.

I started developing my personality and interests during those times of great changes. As a teenager, I also encountered many challenges that helped mold my adult life and guided how to live the rest of it.

I believe that during the years growing up as a teenager, I gained and incorporated some skills, developed positive social traits, built relationships, learned how to take responsibility to communicate effectively, and make distinctions between right and wrong on my own.

My life as a teenager was not so complicated, as in many cases, I was quite simple. I lived my life according to the things that were popular at that time, like the clothes I was wearing, the music I listened to, my hairstyle, and the food I ate.

I had hopes, dreams, and the desire to be loved and respected. I had the opportunity to be who I was, without much interference from other people, especially my parents.

I like to think that my teenage lifestyle had a positive impact on the rest of my life, because I had the tools that I needed to learn, grow, and mature into a well-adjusted human being.

The memories of my father growing up set the bar for the kind of life I wanted for myself once I was married.

I loved my father with all my heart, but thinking back to the time when I was a little boy, and examining very carefully what he had put my mother through, I definitely didn't want to be like him growing up.

Chapter 4

So, I was thirteen, and six years had passed since the debacle of Argentina. But our journey didn't end there. Six years later, when I was a teenager and just starting to find my place in the world, my father's old restlessness returned.

His obsession with immigration flared up again, this time with a new target in mind: Australia.

I was older then, more aware, more skeptical. I had already seen how uprooting a family in the name of a better life could leave scars.

But reason had little effect on my father when he had an idea in his head. He was convinced that Australia was the answer. A land of opportunity. A fresh start. Maybe even redemption for the failure of Argentina.

And so, once again, we packed our lives into bags. This time, I knew what I was leaving behind. Friends, school, the familiar street, and hometown. The things that had begun to anchor me.

Australia was farther, stranger, and more distant than anything I could have imagined. And though we stayed longer than we had in Argentina, it too would not be forever.

The reason we went to Australia was different from the first time. This time, my father had a real connection; his sister was already living there, established and settled.

That made all the difference to him. It wasn't just a vague hope anymore; it was something he could point to, someone who had made it.

It was in January 1963 when we left for Down Under. The ship was Italian, Verdi, and the journey would take nearly a month. I was a teenager by then, almost fifteen years old. Old enough to understand what it meant to start over.

But there was also a strange sense of adventure in it, a kind of resignation mixed with curiosity.

Life on the Verdi had its own rhythm. Days at sea blurred together, but we made the best of it. We befriended some of the workers on the ship, young men mostly, Italian like us, some chasing their own destinies, some just doing a job.

They played cards with us, taught us little tricks to pass the time, and shared stories that made the long voyage feel shorter.

For a while, the open sea felt like a promise. But the truth is, even before we arrived in Australia, I think I knew this wasn't going to be permanent either.

It was as if my father were chasing something that couldn't be found on any continent, some ideal life, some version of success that kept slipping just out of reach.

For a few days, we saw neither land nor any other ship from the time we left. A few days later, it was early in the morning when we reached the Suez Canal.

I took notes as I was learning from someone who worked on the ship about that place. The Suez Canal, 120 miles long, a narrow thread of water bordered by desert and warships, where the heat clung to our skin and the silence was broken only by the groaning of the ship.

Back then, it took that ship almost twenty hours to pass through to finally reach the Red Sea.

We traveled for days before reaching the most memorable stop: Singapore, a place that seemed to buzz even from the deck.

We stayed long enough for passengers to disembark and wander the bustling port, where shops overflowed with duty-free goods–watches, cameras, fabrics, and perfumes.

I felt stepping into another world, vibrant and very strange. For all of us, it was the real taste of the East, and for a brief moment, we forgot how far we still had to go.

Then the ship pushed onward, across the Indian Ocean, towards the unknown future waiting for me on the far side of the world.

There was something else that unsettled me during that voyage, something I didn't fully understand at the time, but couldn't ignore.

My father had grown unusually friendly with one of the women working aboard the Verdi. She was part of the crew, maybe in the kitchen or part of the cleaning staff.

I don't remember exactly, but I remember how often they spoke, how casually he laughed with her. How he sought her out, it wasn't just small talk. I watched quietly, uncertain what to make of it. My mother didn't notice, or perhaps she chose not to.

Even as a teenager, I knew something wasn't right. I felt it in my gut. It was like a shadow cast over the trip, one that would stay with me long after we reached dry land.

All in all, it took us a month; it was February when we finally got to Australia. My father's sister and her husband came to get us.

We left Italy in January. It was winter when we boarded the Verdi, and I remember the cold air biting my face as we waved goodbye to shore.

A month later, when we arrived in Australia, I stepped off the ship into full summer. The heat hit me like a wall, sunburnt sidewalks, bright skies, people in short sleeves.

I had never experienced such a sharp contrast, and it left me both excited and disoriented.

For the second time in my young life, I found myself in a new and strange environment. No friends yet, new school, language barrier, and everything else that came with immigrating to a foreign land.

It was February 1963 when we arrived in Melbourne, stepping off the ship into a world that felt completely upside down.

While our hometown in Italy was still shivering through winter, we were met with scorching sun, dry air, and blinding blue sky.

It was the first time I experienced summer in what was supposed to be winter. That moment alone made me feel like we had landed on another planet.

We settled in a suburb outside Melbourne, near where my father's sister lived. She welcomed us with warmth, and for the first time in a long while, there was a sense of family connection, a tether that helped us feel less like strangers.

My father found work quickly, again in manual labor. My mother adjusted the best she could, even though I could tell her heart was still in Italy.

As for me, I was caught between two worlds. I was a teenager trying to figure out who I was, and once again, I had been pulled out of everything familiar.

I enrolled in school, struggled with the language barrier, and tried to blend in, but it wasn't easy.

I carried the weight of two migrations now, and a growing awareness of the things in my family that weren't being said. That feeling I had on the Verdi, watching my father with another woman, lingered.

I didn't have proof, and I didn't bring it up, but the seed of suspicion had been planted. It would grow slowly, feeding silently off other moments I hadn't paid attention to before.

Despite that, I did find moments of peace, walking alone, learning the new city, watching the strange birds in the trees. I was always trying to ground myself, trying to feel like I belonged somewhere.

But deep down, I think we all knew it wasn't permanent. My father's heart, once again, began to turn back towards Italy.

After five months in Australia, something changed. Not in the scenery or the work, but in the air around our home, something subtle, a shift in mood.

One Sunday morning, while walking with my mother to church under the heavy summer sun, she paused, looked at me, and sighed deeply.

"Son, I can see in your eyes that you miss your friend and your grandparents. Don't worry. Don't make yourself too comfortable here. Soon, your father will change his mind about staying here."

I looked at her, surprised, "Ma, how do you know? Did he tell you that?"

"No, he didn't," she said softly. "But I know him. Just from the way he talks."

"Okay, Ma," I answered. "From your mouth to God's ears."

She was right. Again.

By August, just seven months after we arrived, the decision was made. My father had quietly come to the same conclusion he had reached years earlier in Argentina: this wasn't it.

This wasn't the life he had imagined, and he couldn't pretend otherwise anymore. The difference this time was that I wasn't a little boy; I was old enough to feel the full weight of another goodbye.

There was no celebration, no mourning, just resignation. We packed just once more, said farewell to my aunt and the friends we had managed to make in that short time, and prepared ourselves for the long journey home.

We boarded the same ship that had brought us to Australia, the Verdi. Some of the crew were different, but many were the same.

And among them, so was she-the woman I had watched so closely on our first voyage. The one I suspected had shared more than just polite conversation with my father.

I didn't say anything. Not to him, not to my mother. But I watched. Quietly. Intently. I knew her face by then, the way she moved, the way she smiled at him.

Nothing obvious happened, but I noticed everything-the casual exchanges, the times they were near each other on deck, the looks that lingered too long.

I was just a teenager, but I was old enough to read between the lines.

Once during the trip, I trailed behind my father as he went down towards the lower deck, while my mother remained in the cabin, attending the little ones.

He didn't know I was there. I kept my distance, hiding behind corners, watching him meet her by her cabin. She was there waiting for him.

They spoke in hushed tones. I couldn't hear the words, but I didn't need to. I saw enough. The easy comfort between them, the quiet smiles, the closeness that didn't belong to strangers. A minute later, she pulled him by the hand into her quarters.

I felt sick to my stomach. Not just from what I had seen, but for the fact that I couldn't tell anyone. I carried it like a stone in my stomach.

It wasn't just a betrayal of my mother-it felt like a betrayal of us, of everything we had sacrificed to follow him across the oceans.

The trip back to Italy was different. I wasn't a boy anymore. Something in me had hardened. I didn't confront him. I don't think I could have. I always suspected him of being a womanizer. After that, I never looked at him the same way again.

Looking back now, those journeys-first to Argentina, then to Australia-weren't just about chasing opportunity. They were chapters in a much larger story, one I didn't fully understand until years later.

By then, I had already known for years that my father was abusive towards my mother. His jealousy had no limits. He would accuse her of things she never did, question her every move, and punish her with silence or rage. Yet behind it all, he was hiding something himself.

I saw it with my own eyes. He was a hypocrite. While he kept my mother in fear and submission, he was having affairs, who knows how many. That trip on the Verdi opened my eyes to the double life he was capable of leading.

I made myself a promise. I didn't want to become like him- not in the way I loved, not in the way I treated the woman who would one day be in my life.

I didn't want my future to echo with betrayals. I knew these things about him. I had carried them in silence. What I didn't know-not then-was that the worst was still to come.

Chapter 5

Back in Italy, life picked up where it had left off, but I had changed. I had returned with a broader view of the word-one shaped by two emigrations and the lessons that came with them.

I had learned a few words of Spanish in Argentina and some English in Australia, enough to get by, enough to feel the first stirring of what it meant to live in someone else's culture.

But it wasn't just for the languages that stayed with me. It was the feeling of not belonging, of being uprooted and replanted and replanted again and again.

I had seen how quickly life could shift, how easily people could wear masks. I had witnessed my father's contradictions up close, and I began to understand that being a man-being a good man-meant more than just working hard and providing for your family.

It meant being honest. Being kind. Being accountable. Those weren't lessons he taught me directly. They were things I learned in the silence, in the spaces between his actions and my observations.

Back in my hometown, I carried those silent lessons with me. I wasn't the same boy full of wonder and trust. Something in me had changed, grown more watchful. More cautious. But also, strangely, more determined to find a life that made sense, and to be someone I could live with.

We returned just in time for me to begin high school. I should have been thinking about books, friends, and the normal anxieties of teenage life. But nothing about my path was ordinary.

My father's old obsession resurfaced almost immediately-his dream that one of his sons, preferably me, would become a priest.

It was hope combined with a pressure that sat on my shoulders like a mantle I hadn't chosen.

Without even knowing it, my parents had already made arrangements for a visit.

"Let's go there, and after they give us a tour, you decide," said my father. "I made the appointment yesterday."

We were going to visit the seminary–not as tourists, but with serious intentions.

My parents had already spoken about it in passing, especially my father, who seemed convinced that a life of discipline and faith would shape my future.

I was still too young to argue, too unsure to protest, so I went along quietly, more out of duty than desire.

The seminary was tucked away on a hill outside town, surrounded by tall cypress trees and high stone walls that made it feel like a world apart.

When we arrived, a priest greeted us warmly and began showing us around–classrooms with wooden desks, a library filled with thick Latin volumes, and a modest chapel where the air smelled of incense and old wood.

I could hear distant murmurs of boys reciting prayers behind closed doors. We sat with the Rector in his study, a formal, intimidating room with crucifixes on the walls and books neatly arranged behind glass.

The Rector spoke in a calm, deliberate voice, laying out the rules: early rising before sunrise, prayers before meals, silence during study, no visits home except once a month, and on major holidays.

Strict discipline. Structure. Obedience. I listened to all that, but my heart was already retreating.

After the meeting, as we walked through the corridors, I watched a few of the seminarians moving in a quiet single file.

Their faces looked serious–older than their age, somehow. Not unhappy, but distant, like they had already stepped away from the world I still clung to.

I felt a knot in my stomach, a sense that this place wasn't mine. Not yet.

Outside, I said nothing. My parents spoke softly between themselves, hopeful. But I think my mother noticed my silence.

That night I couldn't sleep. I kept thinking about the long halls, the rules, the stillness. Something in me hesitated, even resisted. But I also knew this: when your parents believe something is good for you–especially back then–you didn't just say no.

I wasn't ready to give an answer. But the road ahead had already begun to unfold.

A few days passed after that first visit to the seminary, and I said very little. I kept everything inside, trying to make sense of what I felt.

It wasn't fear exactly–it was more like hesitation, a quiet resistance I didn't yet know how to name.

At home, my father seemed convinced. He spoke as if the decision had already been made, as if my silence meant agreement.

My mother, on the other hand, moved with a quiet resolve. She didn't pressure me. She simply began preparing.

She had a special kit made for me–sheets, towels, pajamas, underwear, socks. Everything embroidered with my initials in tiny, perfect stitches.

It was the kind of love only a mother shows–practical, thoughtful, and done without asking for thanks.

I remember watching her fold each item with care, as if she were wrapping a part of herself to send with me. I didn't know what to say.

One evening, as she was putting the last few pieces into a small suitcase, she turned to me and asked softly. "Hai paura?"

I shook my head. "No. Solo che…non lo so ancora."

She didn't push. She just nodded and said, "E' normale."

Later that night, my father sat with me at the kitchen table. No lectures this time–just a quiet talk.

He rested his elbows on the table and said, "Felice, faith, discipline, and sacrifice built men of strength and character. Just try it, and if it isn't right, we'll talk again."

"Daddy, I'm willing to try," I said. "I'll do it, not to become a priest, but just to save you money, since it's free."

I say yes! Not out loud, not at that moment. But I had made peace with the idea. Maybe it was the look in his eyes, or the quiet trust in my mother's hands as she packed for me–that made me give in.

And a few days later, I was on the road again–this time not across the ocean, but into a world of silence, prayers, and something I didn't yet understand: the beginning of becoming myself.

The day I entered the seminary, the sky was overcast– fitting, somehow. The road there was quiet, lined with olive trees and low stone walls.

My parents rode with me, both solemn in their own way. My mother's hands rested on the small suitcase she had packed with such care. My father, unusually quiet, kept his eyes on the road.

When we arrived, a bell rang fairly in the distance. The same priest who had shown us around the first time greeted us again.

He shook my father's hand, nodded to my mother politely, and placed a hand on my shoulder. "Benvenuto, Felice. Sei pronto per cominciare?"

I gave a small nod. I wasn't sure I was ready–but I had come.

Inside, the seminary was just as I remembered. The silence was different than at home–heavier, more complete.

Even the floors seemed to absorb sound. The seminarians were already gathered in the chapel for evening prayer. The voices echoed like a chant across the old walls.

I was shown to my dormitory—a simple row of beds, a small locker, bare windows that looked out over the slopes of Monte Oliveto.

I unpacked slowly, placing the carefully embroidered towels and shits in their place, each one a reminder of home, and my mother's quiet devotion.

That evening, I was called to see the Rector—a towering figure, dignified, with kind but piercing eyes. We sat in a small room lined with theological books and portraits of saints.

He asked me questions of which he already knew the answers: about my background, my schooling, my understanding of the faith.

I answered politely, thoughtfully. He listened, hands folded, nodding from time to time.

At the end, he looked at me with calm certainty and said, "Credo che tu abbia la stoffa del sacerdote, Felice. Hai una luce negli occhi."*

I smiled. "Grazie, Padre."

But I lied to him.

Deep inside, I knew I didn't want to become a priest. I admired the dedication, the ritual, the sense of purpose—but it didn't belong to me.

Not really. Still, I said nothing. I nodded respectfully, as expected. Because that's what you did.

I was sixteen. I wanted to be good. I wanted to make my parents proud.

But in my heart, something was already pulling me toward another path—one I hadn't yet found, but I knew I had to follow.

---

*I believe you have the makings of a priest, Felice. There's a light in your eyes.

Chapter 6

So instead of enrolling in a regular high school, I entered the seminary in Airola, the next town over-just five kilometers from home, but it might as well have been a world away.

It wasn't that I was dragged into it kicking and screaming. I was still a good Catholic boy, still serving Mass, still going to confession, still believing-at least on the surface-that this might be my calling.

Or maybe I just wanted to make my father proud. Maybe I thought this was how I could bring peace to our home, most importantly to him, to myself.

But deep down, I already carried questions. Questions about faith, about God, about what it meant to give your life to something you didn't yet fully understand.

And though I didn't know it then, that seminary would not only shape my faith-it would challenge it, and forever change the course of my life.

My father had a practical way of thinking. For him, the seminary wasn't just a path to priesthood-it was a free education.

He used to say, "If you don't want to become a priest, you can always quit before ordination."

It sounded reasonable on the surface, but deep down, it revealed something more. He didn't seem to care much about whether I had a genuine calling.

What mattered to him was discipline, structure, and the status that came with having a son in the clergy.

So, following my father's advice I entered the seminary in September 1963.

I had just turned fifteen, and I entered the seminary with more questions than conviction.

I convinced myself it was temporary, I would see how it felt, and if it wasn't for me, I could always walk away.

But once inside, everything changed. The schedule, the silence, the constant presence of prayer-it was a different world, strict and sacred, but also isolating.

And yet, part of me tried to embrace it. I still believed in God. I still had hope that maybe this was the right path-not because my father wanted it, but because it might help me find answers to the questions I carried since childhood.

But I would soon discover that God wasn't the only force waiting for me inside those walls.

Life in the seminary was orderly, quiet, and deeply structured. We rose early, prayed, studied, ate in silence, and ended the day with more prayer.

The subjects were heavy: philosophy, theology, Latin, scripture. I followed along with quiet diligence, memorizing verses, reciting doctrines, taking notes I wasn't sure I believed in.

I didn't question anything aloud. But inside, I was asking all the time: *Is this really me? Is this where I belong?*

There was little room for wandering thoughts, but they came anyway-especially at night, when the halls were dim and the prayers no longer filled my mind, and that was when I wrote everything in my diary.

The old seminarians moved like ghosts– disciplined and focused, having already surrendered. Some of them seemed at peace. Others, like me, looked at the windows just a little too long.

Weekends were quiet, sometimes painfully so. A walk in the gardens, a rare visit from home, extra time in the library.

We were allowed to see our parents. My mother came to see me, but my father, not so much. I told her I was fine, I was learning, I was adjusting.

But I wasn't.

In truth, I felt like a visitor in someone else's dream. The ritual, the rules, the silence—it all belonged to something noble, yes, but distant from the life I secretly longed for.

I didn't yet know what that life was, only that it wasn't this. Sometimes at night, when the lights were out and the only sound was the rustle of pages or whispering prayers, I would stare at the ceiling and try to imagine my future.

I couldn't picture myself behind an altar. I couldn't imagine taking vows I didn't fully understand. But I also couldn't imagine telling my parents the truth, not yet.

There was still a part of me that thought maybe I'd change. That the calling would come. That in time, belief would take root in the empty space I felt inside.

But instead, something else was beginning. A different voice. A quiet unrest. And soon, a moment that would change everything.

The seminary shared a wall with the convent. Just one wall. On the other side were girls around our age, also studying, also living under rules and silence. We never saw them-not officially. The wall made sure of that.

But I often imagined a door in that wall. Not a real one-just a door I pictured in my mind. A door I could open quietly, step through, and discover something that no prayer or confession could offer: human connection. Curiosity. Maybe even love.

We weren't allowed to speak to the girls, not even to acknowledge them if we happened to pass by during the rare outdoor moments.

And yet, their presence was undeniable—like a hidden pulse behind the stone. It made my heart beat faster in ways I didn't fully understand yet.

I tried to stay focused. I prayed harder, studied more. But something had already begun to stir in me. I was starting to question not only my faith-but also my own heart, and what it truly wanted.

By January 1964, I had been in the seminary for

four months. I was trying to keep my head down, trying to follow the path laid out for me.

But something inside me had begun to shift-quietly, like the change in season, noticeable only if you were really paying attention.

One day, we were told that the seminarians and the postulants from the convent would be taken to a theater in town to watch a religious film: "*Il Vangelo di San Matteo.*" Italian for: "*The Gospel According to Saint Matthew.*"

It wasn't unusual for us to attend religious events like this, but what made this different was the arrangement.

The girls sat on one side of the theater, the boys on the other. Between us, a narrow three-foot aisle-just enough distance to preserve appearances, but not enough to keep our eyes from wandering.

It wasn't meant to be a social event. But we were sixteen. We were human. The silence between our rows felt charged, like a current passing unseen through the air.

We weren't allowed to speak, to smile, or to even glance for too long. And yet, something happened that day-something quiet but unforgettable.

Because somewhere across that three-foot aisle, a pair of eyes met mine. And in that brief moment, everything began to change.

It was a special screening organized for students, religious in nature, meant to inspire.

The auditorium was wide, filled with rows of uniforms, boys on one side, girls on the other. A sea of young faces, quiet chatter, whispers settling into the hush of the screen.

And then…her. So many girls…so much room in that theater. Out of all the places she could've sat, she chose to sit directly across from me–close enough to notice, but just far enough that it still felt like a dream.

Lucia.

Even before I knew her name, something moved in me. There was stillness around her, but her presence pulled at me like a thread.

A glance, a second too long, a softness in her expression– she wasn't just another girl in a convent dress. She was meant to be there. ***Meant to be seen.*** Someone up there wanted me to see her.

Whoever *He* was–God, fate, destiny–*He* left it up to someone else to tell me the truth later.

That she was more than a girl in that theater. That she was the missing piece of a story I hadn't been told. That she was family. Blood. My half-sister.

But on that first day, none of that existed. All I knew was the feeling I'd been struck by something profound, something impossible to name.

It wouldn't be long before I'd learn the rest. But for now, all I had was a look across the aisle, and a strange new sound of my heart speaking a language I had never heard before.

I couldn't help-I tore a corner off the program and scribbled my name, then passed the note to her, my heart thudding like a hammer.

She looked at it, then up at me, and smiled. Then she wrote hers. Her name, Lucia Perrotta. Just seeing her handwriting made her feel more real, more reachable.

Her name, her smile, her presence-they all stayed with me after that brief moment in the theater. And as fate would have it, I soon learned that she was from Rotondi-a town less than two kilometers from mine.

Rotondi wasn't unfamiliar to me. I had friends there. I'd played soccer on its dusty fields, run its narrow streets, and shared laughter with boys I still considered like brothers. But more than that, I had family there-my aunt Maria lived in Rotondi.

Knowing she came from a place that already felt familiar made her presence feel even more intimate, more possible. It was as if the invisible wall between our worlds had grown thinner.

She wasn't some distant figure hidden behind convent walls anymore-she was someone with roots close to mine. Someone I could almost reach.

And yet, we were still just glances and curiosity. Words hadn't yet passed between us. But I could feel it beginning-like a thread quietly pulling us closer, weaving together two lives that had no permission to intertwine.

So, we weren't allowed to speak in the theater, and we certainly weren't given a chance to meet after. But I couldn't let it end there-not with the way she had looked at me. Not with the way something inside me had shifted since that moment.

She could have looked away that morning, and maybe life would've been simpler if she had. But she didn't. She stood there, and in the stillness, the world opened.

At the seminary and also at the convent, we were given one weekend off each month. Just one chance to step out of those walls and breathe air that wasn't part of the Church.

And when that first free weekend came, I knew exactly what I was going to do. On Saturday morning, after taking my dusty bike out of the shed, I pedaled the two short kilometers to her town.

It wasn't far–barely two kilometers–but every turn of the pedals felt like I was crossing a boundary I'd never dared to test before.

I didn't know what I would say or even if I'd find her. But I kept pedaling.

I found the street, her house, and after leaning my bike against the wall, I sat on a stone bench across from it, heart pounding.

I waited and waited, and suddenly there she was. She finally came out, saw me, and recognized me in an instant. Her face lit up in a way I'll never forget.

She wasn't alone. A woman was with her–maybe her mother or her grandmother. When she saw me, her eyes changed, just for a moment, but she made it like she didn't know me. I understood.

They walked into a small market to pick up a few things, and when they passed by me again, she gave me the smallest sign–barely a glance, a flicker of a gesture. Wait.

So I did. I stayed on that bench like a statue, as the sun dipped lower and the breeze picked up. She went into the house with the woman, and I waited.

Minutes passed like hours. I was sure she wasn't coming. But then, just as I was about to stand up and leave, she came out alone.

We couldn't talk at first. Just smiled at each other, and she gave me a sign to follow her. I grabbed my bike and pulled it along, as we walked to the villa just at the outskirts of town.

It was very quiet there. The air smelled of spring grass mixed with stone. That's where we really spoke for the first time. That was where something between us truly began.

For a while, all we knew was the sweetness of seeing each other. We found moments–brief ones, stolen like breath–on monthly breaks or through whispered letters passed through trusted hands.

She was the only real thing in a life that felt scripted by others. At sixteen, I didn't yet know that love could carry a secret so heavy it would change everything.

But the past has a way of surfacing, even when no one speaks it aloud. And when it came, it came quietly, like a whisper behind a closed door.

A truth buried in the lives of my parents, waiting to be uncovered. I didn't realize, but the silence surrounding our families was already shaping us.

The things left unsaid, the names never mentioned, the odd looks from older relatives, it was all part of something larger.

We thought we had found something innocent, something rare and beautiful. But the truth, waiting quietly in the background, had a different story to tell.

The brief encounter wasn't much by ordinary standards. But for two teenagers wrapped in silence and expectations, it felt like the beginning of everything.

We sat on a bench that had been warmed by the sun, exchanging a few words-polite, careful, but charged with something new. Something forbidden and deeply human.

I cleared my throat to start a conversation. "Lucia, after the theater, did you think that you would see me again?"

She nodded. "Felice, I knew you had my name, and you knew where I lived. I thought about you during these few days. I'm happy you came. And here we are."

I sighed. "Lucia, I just couldn't wait to see you. What were your thoughts when you came out of your house and saw me sitting right there, across the street?"

She smiled. "My heart started to beat fast, from the surprise."

"I hope your mother didn't notice anything. Did she?"

She turned to me with sadness. "The woman you saw with me is my grandmother."

"Oh, I see. Does she live with your family?"

"Felice, no, I live with my grandparents."

"About your parents?"

"They're in a better place," she said.

"Lucia, what are you talking about?"

I could detect the sorrow in her face when she said, "My parents died in a car accident right after I was born."

"Lucia, I'm very sorry, I didn't mean to upset you."

"Felice, don't be sorry. You didn't know. It's fine," she said. Then she continued. "Let's talk about us a little bit. I'm curious, are you studying at the seminary to become a priest for real?"

I grinned. "No, Lucia. I'm not going to lie to you. I am not cut out to be a servant of the church. Think about it, if I were for real, would I be here talking to you?"

"I guess not. We have to be very careful, though. Do you know that we're not allowed to have a love relationship while we are there?"

"Yes, I know. What about you, Lucia? Are you in the convent to be a nun? If that is the case, then I am only wasting my time trying to get together with you. Am I?"

"No, I am not there to be a nun, and you're not wasting your time. I'm just there to study and save my grandparents' money for school," she said. "Would I be here with you if that were the case?" she asked, smiling.

I sighed with relief. "Then we can keep on seeing each other, every time we have a break. What do you say, Lucia?"

"I like that. We usually get breaks at the end of each month," she said. "About you?"

"The same, at the end of each month," I replied.

"Okay then," she said. "I would like to stay a little longer, but I have to go. My grandmother is probably wondering where I am," she added, glancing at her watch.

I cleared my throat. "Okay, Lucia, I'll walk you back."

"Thank you."

I got my bike and we started to walk back towards the center of town.

"Lucia, I meant to ask you. Do you know the Casale family?"

"Do you mean Luigi and Maria?"

"Yes, exactly."

"Of course I know them. They live two doors down from us. Why are you asking?"

"Maria is my aunt, my father's sister."

"I know them well. Maria is a very good friend of my grandmother."

"Okay, Lucia, I'm happy to hear that. Let me ask you this. Since we have tomorrow free, can I come back to see you?"

She hesitated for an instant, then said, "I don't know. We usually go to church on Sundays. But I like that."

"Lucia, I'm also busy in the morning. Usually, I go to church to serve Mass. I was thinking after lunch. Perhaps at 2:00?"

"That's perfect. We'll meet right there, in the villa, by the entrance."

We reached the main avenue, and we had to split.

I got on my bike and said, "Very good, Lucia. I'll see you tomorrow then."

I started my run back home, and I was thinking about our conversation. We had spoken quietly, our conversation light but meaningful, like two people learning the rhythm of each other's thoughts.

There was a warmth in her smile that made me forget, for a moment, the walls in the seminary and the convent that separated our worlds.

Before parting, we agreed to meet again–Sunday at 2:00 in the afternoon. A small promise made before she returned to her convent and I to my studies, each of us carrying that shared moment like a folded note hidden in our heart.

I didn't know much about Lucia–not really. I knew her name, the slope of her shoulders, the soft, thoughtful way she held her hands when she wasn't speaking.

I knew that she walked with quiet purpose, like someone who wasn't trying to be seen, but couldn't help being noticed.

While pedaling my way back home, I could stop thinking about her and about a specific moment.

My mind went back in time, a few days after we had seen each other in the theater.

From the seminary, the convent's courtyard and garden could be seen. It was in the afternoon, after the prayers, when I looked out the windows, I saw her at a distance in the cloister garden.

She was alone, standing beside a rose bush that had just begun to bloom. She wasn't picking the flowers, just looking at them, her head slightly tilted, as though she was listening to something only she could hear.

The wind caught her veil just enough to lift it, and it, too, was curious about her. She turned suddenly, like she sensed that I was there watching, and our eyes met.

I thought she might look away, pretending not to have seen me. She didn't, instead she stood there steady and calm, waved at me, and there was something in that look, something illegible, but not disinterested.

I didn't try to hide. I was afraid, if I did, I would break that enchanting moment. I saw the smile she gave me, not as an invitation, nor that she was making a promise by it.

The smile seemed sincere, innocent, but what captured my attention, though, was something else. It was about the way she moved, the way she looked, the way she carried herself.

Everything in her personality felt very familiar, like I was looking at myself in a mirror.

I couldn't explain how two people, two strangers, could have a similar personality. Thinking that I was just fantasizing, I shook my head and went back to study.

Chapter 7

Riding my bike, I got home in time for dinner, and afterwards I went to the usual place to meet my friends. Got back home very late, and as I always did, before going to sleep, wrote about the events of the day in my diary.

After I said my prayers, I lay there on my bed, staring at the ceiling. I couldn't sleep. Her voice, her laugh, the way her eyes softened when she smiled–all of it stayed with me.

The thought of seeing her again so soon filled me with a restless energy, the kind I hadn't felt before. I kept staring at the ceiling, smiling in the dark, as if the stars could hear my heart beating a little faster.

The next morning, I climbed out of bed and stepped barefoot out onto the balcony, the cool tiles beneath my feet waking me up fully.

I looked up at the sky-it was overcast, a heavy blanket of gray stretching across the valley. The air smelled of moisture. I was sure that rain was coming.

My heart sank. If it rained, we wouldn't be able to meet. We didn't have cell phones or an easy way to contact each other. A missed meeting could mean waiting another whole month. The thoughts tightened something in my chest.

Still, I went about my morning routine, trying to push away the worry. I got dressed with care–white shirt, pressed pants– hoping the day would hold.

First, I had to go to church to serve the Mass. That came before anything else. Afterward, I would return home for lunch. And then, if the sky allowed, I would ride to see her.

I stood for a moment before leaving the house, looking once more at the sky. Then I whispered a quiet prayer–not for a miracle, just for the rain to wait.

I got to church and served the Mass as I always did, though my thoughts weren't entirely on the altar. Each time I glanced out one of the tall church windows, I searched the sky.

The clouds were darker now, heavier. The smell of the rain thickened. Still, I clung to hope. On my way back home for lunch, I looked up again. The sky wasn't in my favor.

We sat down at the table–my mother, father, my siblings, and I. I tried to eat, but I could barely keep still. My mother noticed right away.

She narrowed her eyes with a half–smile, folding her napkin slowly like she was building up something.

"Well, on Sundays you usually play soccer in the afternoon," she said, "but you're all dressed up today. Where are you off to?"

I didn't answer right away. I just pursed my mouth in a self-satisfied smirk, but she pressed on with a huge smile. "I know you're not playing soccer. Who is she? Where's she from?"

I could feel the warmth rising to my face. My father just smiled quietly from across the table, fork in hand, not saying a word, just looking. He knew. He'd been there himself, once. He wasn't about to get in the way.

I shrugged, "Ma, you don't know her. I met her in school."

"In school?" she asked. "What school?" she added.

"Ma, I meant…never mind," I said, smiling.

"Be careful not to get in trouble with the Rector at the seminary," my father said. "You didn't forget the rules, did you?" he asked.

"Daddy, I know about the rules," I responded. "If I get in trouble, what can I do? I'll worry about it then."

I was trying to play it cool, but my mother wasn't fooled, while my father was only worrying about me getting in trouble and being expelled from the seminary.

That was the farthest thing from my mind. I was on pins and needles, hoping the sky might clear before two o'clock.

All I could do was finish my lunch, glance out the window, ask my father for money, and keep praying the clouds would show mercy.

As we ate, I tried to keep it casual, but the look on his face told me he knew exactly what the money was for. He reached into his pocket and handed me a few small bills without saying a word of judgment.

"Be careful," he said, giving me a knowing glance. "And don't get into trouble." That was all.

After lunch, I went upstairs to my bedroom, brushed my teeth, and tried to steady my nerves. I stepped out onto the balcony once more, drawn there by habit and hope. To my surprise, the sky had changed.

The heavy gray clouds had begun to lift, giving way to soft blue and streaks of light. A breeze carried the smell of the fresh air instead of rain.

I stood there, silent for a moment, then whispered another prayer-not asking for more, just giving thanks that the day might be ours.

I didn't know what would come of this meeting, but in that moment, the world felt like it was leaning gently in my favor.

I took the bike out of the shed, the tires crunching softly on the gravel as I wheeled it onto the road. The sky above had cleared, and with each push of the pedals, my heart beat a little faster–not from the ride, but from what waited ahead.

Halfway to Rotondi, I stopped at a small bakery. The warm scent of fresh bread and sugar wrapped around me as I stepped inside.

I scan the shelves, uncertain. Finally, I picked out a bag of almond cookies, not knowing if she liked them, only that I wanted to bring her something. A gesture. A sign that I cared.

I arrived at the villa–our meeting place–a little early. The place was quiet, the air still. I leaned my bike gently against the iron fence, then sat on a nearby bench, the bag of cookies resting on my lap.

My eyes searched the path ahead, and my thoughts turned inward, caught between hope and doubt. The world seemed to hold its breath with me, waiting.

And then she arrived.

Lucia walked towards me, her steps light, her expression uncertain at first, then softening into a smile as she drew near.

I stood to greet her, suddenly aware of how tightly I was holding the little bag of cookies.

"I didn't know what you liked," I said, opening it, offering them. "I just thought…maybe."

She laughed, taking the bag gently from my hand. "Almond," she said, opening it and holding one up. "Not bad." She took a bite, thoughtful. "Actually, really good. I love almond cookies."

We sat side by side on the bench, our shoulders not quite touching. The conversation flowed slowly at first–halting, shy.

But soon, something opened between us. She asked about the seminary, why I was there, and what I hoped for.

I looked at her, steady. "I'm not becoming a priest," I said. "That was never my plan. I want a woman in my life. I want a family. The seminary was a way forward–school education. But that path.. It's not the one I'll stay on."

She nodded, quietly, like she had been waiting for me to say that. "I'm not planning to be a nun either," she said. "My aunt is a nun. She teaches at the convent. She helped get me in so I could study. I want to be something more–but first I have to find a way to pay for school."

There it was. The truth–clear, simple, and shared between us. For a moment, the world around us faded: the rustle of leaves, the ticking time.

We were just two young people, each carrying borrowed robes, finally stepping out of them–if only for the length of one honest conversation.

It was only the second time we'd met, yet the ease between us felt like we'd know each other longer–maybe even forever. As we talked, I learned something that made me stop for a moment.

We were born just two weeks apart. Somehow, that detail stuck with me. Not just the coincidence of it, but what it seemed to explain.

I had noticed it before, but at that moment, being so close to her, it was more palpable. It was the way she carried herself–deliberate, thoughtful, always aware–it was like watching myself across the bench.

The way she moved, spoke, even how she carefully brushed crumbs from her skirt after eating a cookie…it all mirrored something familiar. Me.

At that time, I didn't give it much importance. I had just noticed it and filed it away quietly. But deep down, something had clicked.

Our personalities, though distinct, ran along the same current–measured, cautious, but curious. Maybe that's why I felt so comfortable with her. Or maybe it's why I couldn't stop thinking about her.

We talked for what felt like hours, though it was probably less. Time had its own rhythm when I was with her–slower, but more vivid.

Every glance, every shared smile, every small silence between our worlds felt like it carried more weight than usual. Eventually, the hours began to slip away.

Shadows stretched longer on the ground, and the late afternoon breeze carried the chill of the evening. Neither of us said it was time to go, but we both knew.

She stood first, brushing the skirt gently, and I followed. We walked slowly towards where our paths would split—mine towards the road back home, hers towards her own home.

"I'm glad you bought the cookies," she said softly. "Even if you weren't sure."

I smiled. "I'm glad you liked them. Even if you weren't sure."

We laughed, a little shyly. Then we paused.

There was no hug. No dramatic goodbye. Just a glance held a second longer than necessary. A connection not yet taken root that day—not loud, not rushed, but steady and real.

I rode my bike back home, the wind against my face couldn't cool the warmth I carried inside. I didn't know what could come next.

But I knew this much: I'd met someone who, in so many ways, reflected a part of me I hadn't even seen before. And that stayed with me.

It wasn't her face I remembered most of the day—it was her voice. Soft, almost hesitant, like someone walking barefoot into water for the first time.

When we were on the bench, her fingers brushed mine as I handed her a cookie.

"Grazie," she said. Then, after a pause, "You're sure about not becoming a priest?"

It was a simple question, but it stuck with me like a bell. She noticed my ironic expression. Her eyes weren't bold but clear, like she had already guessed my answer before asking it.

"Yes, I'm sure," I said. "I'm not becoming a priest."

She smiled at that, the way someone does when a guess turns out to be right, and said nothing more. But I heard her voice in my head all evening. Not the words—just the way she said them.

Chapter 8

onday came too soon, as it always did. We had no choice but to return—me to the seminary, she to the convent. The brief freedom of the weekend folded back into the quiet, disciplined rhythm of our separate lives.

But something had changed.

In the seminary, our days were built around orders—bells, prayers, meals, and silence.

But I began to notice how I leaned towards the times when we were allowed out: The shared mass, the theater evening, the quiet supervised walks near the convent.

Not because I loved the freedom. I was watching for her. I didn't tell anyone—not even myself at first—that I was waiting. But I was.

Some days she didn't appear at all, and I'd spend the night wondering why. Has she been sick? Was she in trouble? Or had she simply chosen not to come?

Other days, she was there, and those were the days that felt real. Even if we never spoke, even if she barely looked my way, her presence was enough to turn stones into breath.

I had never known someone could become a moment, but Lucia had. She filled the quiet like sunlight fills a window.

From then on, we kept finding each other, every break from studies, every moment when we were home. It was never dramatic, never reckless. Just natural. Consistent. Like something unfolding quietly beneath the surface.

And the more time we spent together, the more I noticed it—the similarities. Not just in the way we spoke or thought, but in how we carried ourselves, how we paid attention to every detail.

It was almost spooky, like watching my own habits within someone else. The same cautious steps, the same reflective silences, the same care in choosing words.

At first, I chalked it up to coincidence. But I'd once read about the law of attraction–the idea that like attracts like.

That people with similar energies and mindsets are naturally drawn to each other.

Maybe that's all it was. Two people on parallel paths, pulled together by some unseen current. I didn't dwell on it too much. It just made sense.

She felt familiar. Not in the way a memory does. And something about that made me feel...less alone.

We didn't talk much about the rules we were breaking. It was as if we both silently agreed that what we had was something separate, something pure, even if it didn't fit the path others expected us to follow.

We walked together through fields just beginning to bloom, sat quietly on stone benches, sometimes not saying much at all.

But in those silences, I felt more certain of her, and of myself, than I ever had during prayers or lectures.

Easter came at the end of March 1964. We had a longer break–a full week, including Easter Monday, which is a holiday in our country.

We had known each other for four months. We had never kissed, not even once. But that was about to change.

That week was different from all the others. There was a quiet boldness between us, a soft current running just beneath the surface.

On the third day of the break, we walked farther than usual, past the olive groves and into a small clearing surrounded by wildflowers.

The sun was warm, but the breeze carried the last chill of winter.

We sat on a low stone wall, our shoulders touching lightly. She looked at me, not shyly as before, but steadily, as if she had made a decision too.

I don't remember who moved first–maybe it was both of us at once. But when our lips met gently, it felt like the most natural thing in the world. Nothing rushed. Nothing stolen. Just a kiss that had been waiting patiently for its time.

After that kiss, something shifted in both of us, silently but unmistakably. We didn't speak about much, but we didn't have to. We saw each other every day for the rest of the Easter break.

The love between us was no longer a possibility or a question. It was real now, solid and present, even if it had to remain hidden from the world around us.

On Easter Monday, I went to see her again. This time, I bought a single red rose. Just one. Not a bouquet–too obvious.

Just enough to say what words couldn't yet risk, and subtle enough not to raise her grandmother's suspicions.

She took it with a quiet smile and held it close, as if it were the most precious gift she had ever received.

During those months, our biggest concern had always been about being caught. We had always told ourselves–and to each other–that we were there just to study.

That was the agreement, unspoken at first, then repeated often enough to feel like a prospective shield. But after that kiss, the truth began to press against the walls we had built.

Love had crept in quietly, and now it stood in full view, making everything else feel more fragile.

There was always a question hovering between us, one I never found the courage to ask: Why are you there? What are you doing there?

Not because she didn't belong in the convent—she did. She carried herself with a kind of inward strength, a quiet that suited that life.

But there was something else, something unspoken or resolved in her. A flicker, a longing. Once I saw her walking with one of the older sisters.

They were speaking softly, and Lucia nodded, but she turned away quickly, wiping at her eyes. It was only for a second. She composed herself fast.

I never asked her what it was. Maybe I should have. But maybe we were both carrying questions the other couldn't answer.

We started asking the kind of questions we had carefully avoided before.

She raised her eyebrows in concern. "Felice, what if someone saw us? What if one of the boys says something to the Rector? Aren't you afraid of getting in trouble?"

We went back and forth, talking in hushed tones while walking on a rural-secondary road.

I shrugged. "Lucia, I'll cross that bridge when the time comes."

She shook her head. "It doesn't take much. One person, just once..."

"Lucia, if they find out, we are both in trouble. You're not concerned about yourself?"

"They won't blame both of us," she added, her voice quieter now. "It's always the boy who gets blamed. You know that. They'll say you led me on. That you—"

"That I corrupt you," I finished for her, trying to smile, though it didn't reach my eyes.

She stopped and looked at me. "Felice, I don't want you to get in trouble because of me."

"Lucia, and I don't want to stop seeing you," I said. "Not now. Not ever, if I'm honest."

She didn't answer right away, but she didn't look away either. Raising her eyebrows, she said, "Let's try not to get caught. Okay?"

I tried to reassure her, but I knew she wasn't wrong. There were rules, expectations, and reputation always ready to fall.

We had broken all of them, and still, neither of us said we should stop.

"Lucia, I'm in love with you. If something happens, don't worry, I'll pay the consequences."

She shook her head. "I love you just the same, or maybe more. Let's stop talking about this right now. I want to enjoy the free month that's ahead of us."

I nodded. "Me too. Lucia, looking forward to it. Next month can come fast enough."

"Just one more week. That's all."

We kept walking, our steps slower than usual. The sun was low, painting the fields gold. We went back and forth like that for the rest of the time together-half in fear, half in hope, always circling the one thing we couldn't say out loud yet: that what we had was with the risk.

Chapter 9

Summer came and brought with it a whole month of freedom from those walls. No bells, no silence rules, no quiet footsteps in the halls.

Just sun-drenched days, long walks, and time—finally for Lucia and me to be together without watching the clock or glancing over our shoulders.

We met every day, as naturally as if we'd always done so. One particular afternoon, half–way already through the vacation, after a walk through the shaded part of the village, I stopped in front of a small coffee shop.

"Come," I said. "Let me buy you an espresso and some cookies."

She hesitated, glancing toward the window. "There are people in there…"

"Just a coffee," I smiled. "Besides, no one here knows us."

"You're right. I don't think anyone here knows me personally."

The coffee shop was small, tucked between the bookshop and the flower vendor's stall, with lace curtains fluttering gently in the open window.

I leaned my bike against the wall. Back then, small towns were safe. She followed me inside. The coffee shop was quiet, cool, the air rich with the scent of ground beans and fresh pastries.

We sat at a small corner table, and for a moment, I watched her without speaking. She looked so at ease in that light–her hands folded neatly on the table, her smile soft but watchful.

"You know," I said, passing her a small plate with two almond cookies, "This feels almost normal."

She looked at me and nodded. "Almost."

She stirred her cappuccino slowly, her eyes watching the spiral of foam dissolving like clouds in water. I remember how quiet she was at first, her fingers nervously tracing the rim of the cup.

Maybe she was waiting for me to speak, perhaps just soaking it in–this strange moment, this almost impossible meeting between a seminarian and a girl of the convent, alone together in a public place.

"I've never done this before," she said finally, her voice low, almost like a confession.

"Me neither," I replied, feeling the weight of the collar I wasn't yet wearing pressing down on me like a question.

We talked for almost an hour. Maybe more. I didn't want it to end.

She glanced outside the window, then at me. "If they find out, I'll be sent away."

"So will I," I said.

She reached across the table, just for a second, and touched my hand. "Then let's remember this," she whispered. "In case we don't get another chance."

It was a hot August day, the kind that shimmered with heat even in the shade. After the coffee shop, neither of us wanted to return to where we were supposed to be.

So, pulling my bike with one hand, holding hers with the other, we wondered, almost without speaking, down a rural road lined with stone walls and olive trees, until we found the river.

The air smelled of dry grass and sun–soaked earth. We sat on the bank, beneath the broad, forgiving shade of an oak tree.

The current moved slowly and clearly, catching the light in silver threads. Sparrows sang somewhere in the branches above, and time softened around us again.

Between whispers and laughter, our fingers found each other. Between kisses and timid touches, our bodies leaned closer, instinctively drawn together like two vines twining towards the same patch of sun.

We were sixteen, still cloaked in the idea of innocence, yet something deeper had awakened–a longing, an urgency we didn't fully understand.

Her head rested on my shoulder. My hand brushed her cheek. There was no one else. Just the sound of the river and the pounding of our hearts.

We came dangerously close–too close. A breath away from crossing a line we could never come back from. But something, perhaps grace, held us back.

A sudden gust of wind shook the tree, as if to remind us. And we stopped. Thank God we stopped.

She looked at me, eyes wide, not with shame, but something like awe. As if we'd both stepped to the edge and looked down–and chosen, just barely, not to fall.

Lucia smoothed her dress, cheek flushed, hair slightly tousled from the breeze under the oak. I stood and offered her my hand, and walked slowly back towards town, the sun now hanging lower, casting long shadows across the fields.

A quiet stream of questions and answers passed between us–not all spoken aloud. *What were we thinking? Would we do it again? What did it mean?*

There was no regret, only the fragile awareness that something sacred and dangerous had brushed up against us. We spoke carefully, like walking barefoot on gravel–tentative, exposed.

As we reached the edge of town, the noise returned: bicycles on cobblestones, voices from open windows, the scent of dinner starting to simmer. And then, turning onto her street, we both froze.

There, stepping out of a dark blue Fiat, were my Aunt Maria and Uncle Luigi. My heart skipped. Lucia's hand tightened around mine before she let go.

Aunt Maria, ever watchful, caught sight of us immediately. She smiled–her usual warm smile–but I knew she'd already taken in the situation: the late hour, the fact that we were walking side by side, the flush in our faces.

Lucia took a step back, like she suddenly remembered her veil wasn't on. But I stepped forward with confidence, as if we had nothing to hide. "Zia Maria! Uncle Luigi!" I called out, arms open.

I kissed them both on the cheeks, the way we do in Italy–left, then right–warm, respectful, familiar. My aunt smelled of lavender and starch. Uncle Luigi gave me his usual nod and half–smile.

Lucia smiled politely. "Buonasera, signori Casale."

There was a pause, short but thick with meaning. Then Aunt Maria looked at me with a glint in her eye. "Felice, vieni…walk with us a bit. Tell us how seminary life is treating you."

Lucia offered a quiet goodbye, her voice barely above a whisper. She didn't look at me as she turned and walked the last few steps towards her house.

I watched her go, her figure retreating into the soft golden light of the evening, until the door closed behind her.

Aunt Maria stood beside me, silent for a moment. Then, almost too casually, she adjusted her purse on her arm and turned to me.

"Is your father home?" she asked, eyes still on the corner where Lucia had disappeared.

"I think so, it's Sunday. He should be," I said, unsure. "Why?"

She didn't answer right away. Just gave a small nod, almost to herself, and said, "Tell him I want to talk. He'll understand."

I didn't understand–not then. There was no scolding, no accusation in her voice. Just something deeper. Knowing. A quiet gravity. I said goodbye to her and Uncle Luigi and made my way home riding my bike.

The warm breeze now felt heavier somehow, like it carried more than just dust and scent. As I pedaled, I kept thinking about Lucia; her eyes as she said goodbye, the way she'd pulled her hand away when she saw my aunt.

And now, the way Aunt Maria had asked that question, as if she already knew everything. Of course she did. They lived just two doors down.

She had known Lucia since she was born. And she'd always had that way of seeing right through me.

Still, I didn't realize, not fully, that she had known the secret. That she had seen something unspoken between us, and carried it in silence.

When I got home and told my father that Zia Maria wanted to talk, he didn't ask questions.

He just nodded and muttered something about the land– "Sara' per la terra..sempre per la terra,"* he said, half to himself.

That was the ongoing issue between him and his sister since my grandparents had passed. Boundaries, inheritance, old family lines tangled in pride.

So, to my relief, and maybe to my shame, neither he nor my mother suspected anything about me seeing Lucia.

We had dinner that evening as we always did. My mother brought the food to the center of the table. My father poured the wine.

---

* "It will be for the land... always for the land."

I answered their questions about seminary life, about the Latin classes, about whether I'd seen the archpriest, Don Paolo, lately.

I played the part calmly and politely. But my mind was somewhere else, still sitting under that oak tree by the river.

Later, when the doorbell rang and Aunt Maria and Uncle Luigi came, I didn't stay to hear anything.

I excused myself, went upstairs to my room, washed my face, changed my shirt, and slipped out the back, heading towards the cafe where my friends and I always met.

Laughter, cards, and the clink of coffee cups. It was a good distraction.

It worked, for a little while. But the surprise came the next day. Not loud, not dramatic. Just silence.

Chapter 10

I came home late that night, the street mostly empty, the breeze cooler after the sun had finally given up the day. The voices of my friends still echoed in my ears, laughter, teasing, talk about nothing and everything.

But beneath it all, I carried the weight of the afternoon, of Lucia's touch still faint on my skin, of the way she disappeared behind her door without turning back.

Upstairs in my room, I changed into my pajamas, opened the window, and sat at my desk with the little lamp casting a pool of yellow light across the page.

I reached for my diary, the worn leather cover soft from use, and began to write, slowly, carefully. I didn't write everything, not exactly.

I never did. Just enough to hold onto feeling. Just enough to make the moment real, in case memory failed me one day.

I lay on the bed and fell asleep late, with my diary still open beside me and my thoughts somewhere along that riverbank.

The next morning, sunlight was already streaming through the window panes when I finally stirred. I came down to the kitchen where my mother was already moving around, her hands busy but her eyes distant. My dad had already left for work.

She placed breakfast in front of me: Pane Tostato, some jam, and a hard–boiled egg. All the same.

But her silence wasn't. She looked…sad. Not angry. Not suspicious. Just…subdued, like someone who'd heard something they didn't quite know how to say.

"Grazie, mamma. I love you," I said.

She nodded with a faint smile, "I love you too, son," she said, but didn't meet my eyes.

She didn't mention Aunt Maria. She didn't ask me where I'd been. And I, not wanting to break whatever thin peace there was between us, said nothing either.

But something had shifted. I felt it. Like the house itself was holding its breath.

I grabbed my bike and went to meet Lucia, like we'd agreed. Same place, same time. But she wasn't there.

I waited five minutes. Ten. An hour. She never came. The next day–nothing.

And the next–it was as if she'd vanished into the air itself. No sign of her, no whispered notes. No familiar footsteps on the sidewalk.

The window she used to look out from remained shuttered. Gone. No explanation. No goodbye. Just the silence.

And somewhere in it, I began to feel what I hadn't understood the day before: Someone had found out about us. And that someone had made sure she was gone from my life.

I had been at the meeting place for three consecutive days, no sign of her. There were a couple of days left of vacation before I had to go back to the seminary.

I thought perhaps the girls had to go back earlier than we boys did. So, the next morning, I got on my bike, heart already tight in my chest, and I took the familiar path towards the convent, five kilometers away.

We had always been careful, Lucia and I. We never met at the gates, never near where the sisters could see. But that day, I went straight to the courtyard, certain I'd find some trace of her.

A sign. A message. Anything. No one there. The place felt colder than usual, like something had been sealed off.

All windows were closed. Not just the shutters, but the curtains behind them, too, drawn like a final curtain on a stage we'd shared for only a few brief scenes.

I waited. An hour passed. Then two. I walked around to the garden wall, the one we used to talk across when no one was watching. Nothing.

I had thought wrong; the girls were not yet back in the convent. But in the silence, I began to understand: someone had intervened.

Quietly. Firmly. Effectively. And I had no way of reaching her.

Three days had passed. Each one heavier than the last. My diary had already absorbed the truth I couldn't speak aloud: *"I can't find her. She's gone. No one will tell me why."*

I retraced every step we'd taken. I went to the river. I walked past her house. I even lingered near the church she went to with her grandmother.

No whisper. Not even a note. Days passed. Then a week. No Lucia.

She had vanished from the few places our paths might have crossed—not at the villa or even at mass. I tried not to imagine her absence as punishment.

I told myself maybe she was sick, or the convent had tightened its rules. But in my heart, I knew something had happened.

While passing Aunt Maria's house, something twisted in my chest. Her visit. Her silence. Her careful words to my father. It had to be her.

She had to have said something. Done something. But it had to be for a good reason. Us having a relationship while attending the seminary and the convent couldn't be the reason. It had to be something deeper.

Then, with every turn of the pedals, my thoughts shifted to my mother's face. Since Aunt Maria's visit, my mother had changed somehow.

Her face, her quiet sorrow, it was like she was carrying the weight of a truth she didn't want to put down in front of me. Why?

The fourth morning, I came down late, and my father was already gone to work. Again, the house was quiet except for the clink of a spoon in the coffee cup.

My siblings were playing in the backyard. It was just the two of us. My mother sat at the table. Unusual for her. Her apron was still on, breakfast already waiting for me, and so was my mother.

"Buongiorno mamma," I said, my voice low, as I kissed her cheek.

She didn't answer right away. She just looked at me–really looked at me–with the kind of eyes that see not just where you are, but what you're carrying inside.

I sat down, she stirred the sugar in her coffee more than once, then set the spoon aside.

"Son, I know what's wrong," she said.

My heart stalled.

She didn't look angry. She looked…tired.

"You're looking for her," she continued.

I didn't speak. I didn't need to.

She nodded slightly, as if confirming something to herself. "I wasn't going to say anything to you. When Maria came last Sunday…"

Her voice faltered, then steadied again. "She said that it wasn't right. That it needed to be stopped before it ruined everything."

I clenched my hand under the table. "Ruined what, Ma? So, was it Aunt Maria who made them take her away?" I asked, all confused.

She started to cry. "No, she came here to warn us about the potential disaster. Anyway, your father, being so busy working, didn't get a chance. But he planned to tell you everything himself on Sunday."

"Maria also spoke to Lucia's grandmother. Quietly. She wanted to protect you, and her," she said.

I narrowed my eyes. "Ma, protect us from what? From each other?"

My mother's eyes filled with tears. "Exactly. She didn't mean to be cruel. She's just…thought it was for the best."

"For the best?" I asked.

I pushed my chair back and stood. "She didn't even let us say goodbye. When she wanted to talk to me on the side."

I stood there, barely breathing, the words not yet formed, when my mother's voice stopped me.

"My son, don't blame your aunt, and what she did is not because you and Lucia broke the convent's rules."

"So, Ma, why don't you tell me why she did it, exactly?"

"Okay, Felice…there's something else you need to know."

I turned slowly, and what I saw in her face–grief, fear, shame–froze me.

"She's not just a girl you met," she said softly. "Lucia…she's your half-sister."

The words landed with a thud, silent but shattering. My mind reeled, trying to understand.

"No," I whispered. "No, that's not–"

"She was born two weeks after you were," my mother said, her voice trembling.

"From a woman your father knew at the same time he was dating me. No one talked about it. It was…hidden. The family took care of it quietly. She has an aunt, who is a nun, but she was raised by her grandparents."

I dropped back in my chair, making it groan. The room suddenly too bright, the air too thin.

"That's why Aunt Maria intervened," she continued. "She recognized her right away. She lives just two doors down, remember? Maria and Lucia's grandmother are best friends. She'd known everything from the beginning. When she saw you together…she didn't say it to you because she didn't know how. But she knew she had to stop it. Now you know."

My mother reached across the table, her hands hovering near mine.

"I didn't want you to find out like this," she said. "But I couldn't let you keep looking for her, not knowing the truth. Not knowing what could have happened."

I couldn't speak. Couldn't cry. My whole body was locked between disbelief and shame, flooded with memories now laced with something unbearable.

The kisses. The closeness. The feeling that had felt so pure…now turned to ash.

I sat in silence, trying to piece together a life that had suddenly been rewritten. My mother's voice came again, softer now, as if speaking to a boy far younger than sixteen.

"Your father didn't have the courage," she said. "He always said he would tell you when you turned eighteen. As if waiting would make it easier."

She looked away for a moment, pressing her fingers to her lips before continuing.

"As for Lucia…the family told her her parents had died in an accident. They raised her in that belief. The plan–if there ever really was one– was to tell her the truth when she turned twenty one."

I felt like the floor had dropped beneath me. Lucia and I. Two weeks apart. Born into parallel lives that almost touched the edge of something terrible.

"But how, Ma…" I managed to say. "How could we be born so close together? He was with you. He married you."

My mother's hands folded in her lap. Her voice trembled.

"I'll tell you everything," she said. "I promise to tell you the truth. Just give me a few minutes to recover."

There was no comfort in her promise–not yet. But there was something in her eyes. A kind of shame laced with love.

She had been hurt, too. But still she sat there, holding the weight of it all so I wouldn't have to carry it alone.

Outside, church bells rang the hour. Inside, my world was no longer the same.

My mother collected herself, kept her eyes on the table as she spoke, the words slow and deliberate, like she'd carried them too long and now they were cutting their way out.

"Your father," she said, "was seeing us both. Me…and Lucia's mother."

I sat still, barely breathing. "Go on, Ma, take your time," I said.

"We were engaged. The wedding was set for December 1947. I remember it was a cold evening– two days before the ceremony. We were having dinner with my parents and my sisters, all of us excited, talking about flowers, guests, the meal…"

Her voice caught, and for a second I saw her not as my mother, but as the young woman she once was–full of hope, just on the edge of becoming someone's wife.

"There was a knock at the door. My sister answered it. I heard voices, then footsteps. A woman walked in…and with her, a young woman, maybe twenty-five. They were strangers. But she said my name. Sat down like she had every right to be there. And then she said: 'I thought you should know…my daughter is one month pregnant with his child.'

"I stared at my parents, stunned. The room felt colder. The first thing that went through my mind was to call off the wedding," she said.

"But I hadn't told anyone something yet…something I had just found out the day before. I only told my two sisters. I was also pregnant. With you."

She looked at me then. "That's why I stayed," she said.

The silence after that was long and crushing. I could feel the walls of the house holding in decades of secrets.

"Your grandfather–your father's father–took care of it. He gave that woman money. A lot of it. Enough to disappear, to raise the child elsewhere. She agreed. Believe me when I say she had no choice. She was sent to live with relatives in another province. She gave birth, but for some reason, she died giving birth to Lucia. The grandparents raised Lucia as their own. Told her her parents had died in an accident."

"And my father?" I asked, barely recognizing my own voice.

"He married me," she said, "with a smile on his face like nothing ever happened."

"Ma, Aunt Maria knew about it from the beginning?" I asked.

"Of course, she's your father's older sister. Thank God. Can you imagine what could have happened if she didn't?" She asked.

I managed to say, "Ma, can you imagine how I would have felt right now, if I had sex with my half–sister?"

"Thank God you didn't." Said my mother, fighting her tears.

I was furious, to say the least. I grabbed my bike and rode to Aunt Maria's house, who probably knew where Lucia was.

I had to know exactly how things were, and who better than my aunt could have told me.

The rain had begun as a soft drizzle, but by the time I was halfway to Rotondi, it felt like the sky was mourning with me.

My legs pumped furiously against the pedals, not because I wanted to arrive quickly, but because I needed to outrun the storm inside me.

The cold wetness clung to my clothes, my hair dripping into my eyes, but I didn't care. I barely noticed the ache in my knees or the bite of the wind in my face.

When I finally turned onto the familiar narrow path to my Aunt Maria's house, the wheels of my bike kicked up a thin spray of mud.

I dropped it by the gate without even looking back and ran up the steps, heart pounding–not from the ride, but from the weight of the questions I carried.

She opened the door before I could knock, as if she had been expecting me. Her eyes widened at the sight of me, all wet, chest heaving, my lips trembling from something deeper than the cold.

"Felice! Dio mio, what happened? Come inside!"

I stepped in, water pooling beneath my sneakers. I could hardly speak. My voice broke in my throat. "You knew… didn't you? About Lucia… about who she really is?"

Aunt Maria's expression faltered. She didn't ask what I meant. She only looked at me with a sadness I hadn't seen in her eyes before.

She gestured towards the bathroom, but I didn't move. She stepped away for a minute and came back, handing me a towel. "Dry your hair, then we'll talk," she said.

"Did you tell her?" I asked while drying my hair. "Did you tell her grandparents? Did she know… before I did?" I asked as we both sat at the kitchen table.

The rain that was tapping gently on the windows had stopped, and now there was a short silence between us. Aunt Maria sat, and her shoulders sagged.

"There are things you deserve to know," she said, her eyes welling. "Things someone should have told you long ago."

"Now I know everything. I just wish I had known about it much earlier," I said.

"It wasn't my place, Felice," she responded softly. "It wasn't my responsibility to tell you. That should've come from your parents… perhaps your father, if he had the courage."

Her words struck me – sharp, but not cruel. Just true. "I knew," she went on. "I knew from the beginning. And yes, your mother, too. She came to me the other day, in tears, after I told them about you and Lucia, when I came to your house on Sunday. She didn't know what to do. She was devastated. I'm glad she finally spoke. Now you know."

I was still drying myself with the towel. I raised an eyebrow. "Did Lucia know?" I asked, almost afraid of the answer.

Aunt Maria shook her head slowly. "Not at first. Not until I saw the two of you together," she said. "Once I told her grandparents they had no other choice than to tell her."

"Why weren't we told before?" I asked, "This would have never happened."

Her eyes welled up. "Because no one expected the two of you to meet. Because no one had the courage to speak. They wanted to wait until you were at least twenty-one."

"Can this be the reason my father wants to immigrate? Perhaps, to take me away from the place he sinned? I can't believe it."

Her voice was soft, almost hesitant, as though she too understood what the words would cost.

"Aunt Maria, my mother told me everything. Just tell me where she is, please," I said. "Is she okay? That is all I need to know for now."

"She's shut herself away, Felice," she said. "Her grandparents are upset. And your father…well, he's made a mess of it. Without meaning to."

I didn't need to ask what she meant. It had been a misunderstanding, yes—but more than that, it had been a breach of something delicate and unspoken.

A spark mistaken for scandal. A moment we hadn't even fully lived now turned into something we had to defend.

Aunt Maria asked me to wait; she walked two doors down to arrange a meeting. She said it would help clear things.

I waited there patiently, and a few minutes later, she was back. She smiled. "Her grandparents want peace. But you have to be the one to speak when we go there. We can go now, they say."

"Okay, I know what I have to say," I replied. "I'll go by myself, you don't have to come," I said, and I left.

I remember entering the walk into their house in Rotondi that morning. I was sixteen, but I felt much younger.

The door opened before I could knock. Lucia's grandmother stood there with a tired face and folded hands.

Lucia wasn't in the room when I entered. I spoke first to her grandparents, who sat quietly at the edge of the sofa. I said I hadn't known what I'd done wrong.

I apologized to them for any shame and confusion. I said it wasn't her fault—not hers, not mine—but if they needed someone to take the blame, I would.

I heard a noise coming from behind; it was Lucia coming out of her room.

She didn't look at me at first. Her eyes were red, her posture straighter than I remembered, like she had built a wall inside herself and was still standing behind it.

I said her name.

She didn't speak—not right away. But after a long silence, she looked up. There was no anger in her face. Just a kind of sorrow, the kind that makes you wish you could go back in time and pause everything before it broke.

"I knew they would misunderstand," she said. Her voice didn't tremble. "But I didn't think it would feel like this."

There was nothing I could do but nod. I wanted to say it hadn't been wrong—what we had shared, the way we had looked at each other, the quiet knowing between us. But in that moment, words would've only deepened the wound.

We were not punished, not formally. No one raised their voice. But when I left that house, I knew something had ended.

Not because we had done something terrible, but because the world around us didn't know how to hold something that fragile, something that sacred.

Chapter 11

When I got home, I told my mother everything, and once I was done explaining, she didn't look at me. She just stood, quietly clearing the table, the sound of dishes stacking gently, the only noise between us.

I sat there for a long time.

The truth didn't come with thunder. It came quietly, like a key turning in a door I hadn't known was locked.

When Aunt Maria told me what had happened, how my mother, perhaps meaning well, had spoken to Lucia's grandparents, I felt the ground tilt.

Suddenly, everything that had been tender and hidden between us had been dragged into the open, interpreted, and judged. Not by us, but by them.

I felt ashamed, not of what had passed between me and Lucia, but of how little I had been able to protect it.

The worst part wasn't that she was gone from view. It was knowing *why.* She had closed herself inside the convent not from conviction, but from hurt.

From fear. From the pressured glares that saw sin where there had only been longing.

And I—I had been in the dark. While she suffered the weight of assumptions and whispers, I had still been hoping to see her in passing, still wondering what I'd done wrong.

Now I knew. And the knowledge burned. I wanted to go to her, to explain, to say: *I didn't ask for this either. I didn't mean for it to become something others had to fix or silence.*

But I also knew she had already paid the price I hadn't. She had been blamed in ways I hadn't. She had been alone in ways I hadn't known.

For days, I walked through Paolisi like a stranger in my own life. The seminary felt cold. The streets were quieter. I found myself looking for her even when I knew she wouldn't be there.

There are wounds that don't bleed but stay open. That week, I learned what it means to carry one.

The man I'd called Papa'–stern, proud, traditional–was now someone else. He had betrayed not just my mother, but me.

He had allowed his own children, born weeks apart, to grow up in separate worlds as strangers. And worse–he had watched, in silence, as Lucia and I unknowingly drifted into something dangerously close to love.

He knew that it would have been probable. And did nothing about it.

For days, I couldn't look him in the eyes. I couldn't listen to his voice without hearing the lies beneath it. And yet…he still sat in his chair at dinner, still stirred his espresso like always, still asked about my studies like nothing had changed.

But everything had changed.

I began to ask quiet questions, digging through old drawers. I looked for photos, letters, anything that could tell me more about the woman he had betrayed, along with my mother. Lucia's mother.

No one in the family ever spoke her name. Not even my mother remembered it. Just that she was from a nearby village. Pretty. Poor. Alone.

One day, I asked my Aunt Maria. She looked at me, long and hard. Then she said, "You're better off letting her rest in peace. She suffered enough."

But I couldn't let it go. Maybe I was guilty. Maybe it was the ache left behind by Lucia's absence. But I needed to know the woman who had been paid to disappear.

The woman who had carried Lucia in silence, who had let her go. I never found her name. But in a drawer at the back of my father's old desk-stuffed under papers and yellowed receipts, I found a letter. Torn, half–burned. Only the bottom remained.

But the words were clear enough to pierce me. The letter was addressed to my grandfather, who had paid the woman to disappear.

These are the words, barely readable; *"He said he loved my daughter. Then he gave her money and shame. Tell him that his daughter has his eyes. He'll never see her."*

I sat there, holding the scorched paper, and realized something simple and terrible. I went to Rotondi to show the piece of that letter to my aunt Maria.

I asked her if she knew anything about it. She nodded, confirming that she was the one who, years ago, delivered it to my grandfather.

Lucia's grandmother had asked her to deliver it, after her daughter had given birth to Lucia and died.

The story didn't begin with Lucia and me. It began long before us; we were just the ones who stumbled into its ending.

There was only the weekend left before I was expected to return to the seminary. My books were still stocked in the corner of my room, untouched since the day at the river. But something in me had shifted. Something irreversible.

I had always felt out of place there. The silence, the rituals, the weight of obedience, they all pressed too tightly against a part of me that longed to breathe, to ask questions, to live freely.

I had convinced myself it was the right thing, the noble path. But deep down, I had never been at peace with it. Now, with everything I had learned, it seemed laughable to imagine returning.

Lucia's aunt, the nun, surely knew. And if she knew, then the Rector knew too. It was only a matter of time before a letter arrived, or I'd be called into his office, that same cold look in his eyes, and told I was no longer welcome.

Oddly, I didn't fear it. I welcomed it. For the first time, I had the clarity to see that this life I was being shaped for–was not mine.

I told my mother that evening, over dinner. My father hadn't come home yet.

"Ma, I'm not going back," I said, steady and quiet. "I've decided I want to enroll in college instead. A regular one."

She didn't argue. She didn't look surprised. Instead, she placed her hand on mine and said, "I think that's the right choice. I actually never agreed. I know the life of the priest is not for you."

And in that moment, I felt something close to relief. Not happiness–not yet. There was still too much grief shadowing the day. But a weight had lifted. A direction had appeared.

Lucia was gone. A truth had been laid bare. But I was still there. Still young. Still standing at the beginning of something unknown, and for the first time, it would be my path to choose.

On Monday, I didn't go back; instead, I went to Benevento to enroll to study engineering. A four-year course.

It didn't take long before the letter came from the seminary. I knew I expected it. It was folded, stamped, and as cold as the seminary walls themselves. *"You have been expelled!"*

No explanation. No hearing. Just a line drawn beneath my name and theirs. I smiled when I read it.

I enrolled at the engineering school. My classes wouldn't begin for another week. But I had no intention of waiting idly for life to resume.

There was something I had to do first–something I had to face, no matter how difficult.

I needed to see Lucia again, this time alone. Just the two of us face to face. Not to chase what had been. That was gone. But to clear the shadow. To say things to her that I couldn't say while others were present.

To speak plainly. To let her know: *"I see you. I know who you are. And you are my blood. From now on, you are a Falzarano!"*

One more time, I had to turn to the one person who had held the key all along. Aunt Maria.

At first, she was hesitant. She didn't think it was a good idea. But I think a part of her knew she owed us that meeting. Maybe she even wanted it, in her own way.

She made the arrangements quietly, with the cooperation of Lucia's aunt, the nun.

Lucia had a short break from her studies—a weekend break visit from her guardians, the same relatives who had raised her under the lie of loss. Her grandparents.

Aunt Maria contacted everyone discreetly. She asked them if, instead of them, I could go to see her. They didn't object. The day came, warm and still, like the world itself was holding its breath.

I dressed in a tracksuit and sneakers. I took my bike out of the shed and pedaled the five kilometers without taking a breath.

We met in a quiet garden behind the convent. No bells, no onlookers. Just a bench beneath a fig tree and the two of us, no longer innocent, no longer guessing.

When I saw her, my heart clenched. She was thinner. Her eyes looked older. But she was still Lucia—still the girl from the riverbank, from the cinema, from those moments that had changed everything.

She looked at me, unsure whether to smile or cry. I sat beside her. We didn't speak at first. Then I said, "Lucia...I know."

She looked away.

I looked into her eyes. "I know who you are. And you need to know that I don't blame you. Not for anything. You are my sister. You always will be."

Her hands trembled in her lap. "I didn't know either, Felice. Not until after that day. They told me...everything. I didn't believe them. I didn't want to. But they showed me letters, photographs."

I nodded, swallowing the ache. "I would give anything for things to have been different."

"So would I," she whispered.

We sat there, the silence no longer cruel, but full of what we didn't need to say. Grief. Forgiveness, and something deeper–recognition.

I reached out for her hands, gently. "For what it's worth," I said, "I'm happy to be your brother."

She looked at me then, tears in her eyes. "I'm proud too."

We stayed on that bench for nearly an hour, speaking in low voices. No longer as the boy and girl on the brink of something forbidden, but as brother and sister–joined not by choice, but by truth.

Before I left, I made her a promise. "I'll visit you," I said. "As often as I can. As your family. No other way."

She nodded, slowly, the way someone does when they want to believe it's possible, even if their heart is somewhere else already.

"I'd like that," she said. "But Felice…I think I know where I belong now."

There was no bitterness in her voice, no trace of regrets–just a quiet certainty that stung deeper than any goodbye.

"I'm staying," she said. "I'm going to take my vows."

It hit me like a stone dropped in water–expected, yet final. Her words rippled through everything we had once imagined, now swallowed by a future neither of us could change.

"You don't want a different life?" I asked gently.

She shook her head. "Not anymore. After everything…this is the only place I feel peace. How can I trust any man after what I've learned?"

I understood then. The convent wasn't her prison–it was a refuge. A place where she could carry the weight of her past, of our story, and lay it at the feet of something greater than both of us.

Sometimes, I would catch her glancing away before I could meet her eyes, and I often wondered what she was thinking.

Was she afraid, like I was? Did she feel this unspoken thing between us? I never knew. And maybe that was part of what made her unforgettable.

We stood. She reached up and touched my cheek lightly, like a goodbye without saying it.

She sighed. "You were the only person I have loved," she said. "And now you're the only family I have that truly sees me."

I wanted to say so much in return. But all I could manage was, "Take care of yourself, Lucia."

"I will," she said. "And you–go live. You have that chance."

I walked away slowly, not looking back. I knew if I did, it would undo me.

In the years that followed, I kept my promise. I visited her once in a while, never too long, always respectful. She smiled when she saw me.

We spoke like family–sometimes laughed, sometimes sat in silence. But there was always a wall, and I respected it.

By then, I had already begun to build my own life. She remained a part of my past–a quiet ache, a tender memory, a chapter I would regret, even though it ended before it ever began.

Chapter 12

The Sunday after, I went to church early to serve Mass. It was something I had done a hundred times before, but that morning felt different. Heavier.

As I stood at the altar, reciting the prayers, helping the archpriest with the chalice and paten, I felt the burden in my chest growing tighter.

Not just the weight of what had happened, but of everything I didn't understand, everything I couldn't undo.

After Mass, while in the sacristy removing my cassock, I turned to the archpriest. "Padre," I said, barely above a whisper, "I need to talk to you."

He looked at me with tired but kind eyes and nodded. We sat down in the wooden chairs near the back, under a faded painting of the Madonna.

"I have to confess," I said. "Everything."

And I did.

I told him about Lucia. About the river. About how close we came to something we didn't even know was wrong.

I told him about the truth—about who she was, and who I was.

I told him about the shame, the anger, the sorrow. About the seminary. The expulsion. My mother. My father. All of it.

When I finished, I looked at him and said, "I probably committed every sin. I don't know what I'm guilty of, but I feel it everywhere."

He didn't interrupt. He just let the silence rest between us for a while.

Then he said, "Felice, life isn't always black and white. Sometimes God allows two souls to cross paths, not to unite them, but to wake them. What you did…was not evil. It was human. You sought the truth. You didn't run from it. That's not sin, that's courage."

I felt my throat tighten.

"But I want to repent," I said. "If not for what I did…then for what I almost did."

He nodded.

So I confessed formally. Not just to the Church, but to myself.

And when he gave me the absolution, I felt not as a clean slate, but as permission to move forward. I walked out of the sacristy lighter than I had been in weeks. Not innocent. Not proud. But forgiven.

The confession didn't erase my past, but it changed how I carried it.

For the first time, I understood something I hadn't before: that faith wasn't about perfection. It wasn't about silence, obedience, or fear. It was about facing the truth, even when it hurt.

After that Sunday, I didn't stop believing. But I stopped pretending.

I no longer looked for God in marble statues or memorized prayers. I looked for Him in honest moments–in the warmth of a friend's voice, the quiet between pages of study, the light slanting through the open window.

But Lucia was never far from my thoughts. Not in a romantic way anymore, something deeper than that.

A connection I carried quietly, privately. I didn't speak of her to anyone, not even my closest friends.

But every so often, I would visit. And every so often, I would kneel in a quiet church, not out of guilt, but to whisper thanks.

For the strange, painful, beautiful path I had walked. For having survived it. For being changed by it.

That season of my life taught me the most important lesson I've ever learned: Love, even when forbidden, leaves behind something sacred. And truth, even when it breaks you, sets you free.

It was September 1964 when I started classes at *"The Industrial Technical Institute"* of Benevento. I had officially just turned sixteen.

It was my first year there, and I made myself a promise: no distractions, no detours. Just focus.

Engineering felt like another world entirely: equations and blueprint physics. Something grounded. Something solid. It was exactly what I needed. I threw myself into the work.

It was aeronautical engineering, one of the most challenging programs in the faculty.

The statistics were grim. Older students warned me constantly about the attrition rate. "Half of you won't be here next year," one professor had said bluntly on the first day.

But I had something most of them didn't: Fire in my chest. Not the kind of burn wild–but the slow, steady kind that comes after you've walked through something painful and survived.

While going to school, I rarely saw my father during the week. It was on a Sunday morning, when I knew he would be home, that I decided to have a talk with him about Lucia.

After getting dressed, I stood outside the balcony staring at the morning light. It was about the end of September, and the mountain air was cool.

My house was literally at the foot of the mountain. The fresh breeze coming from there reminded me that we were in Autumn, with its cold days. And that soon, I would have seen the same mountain top covered in snow.

From where I stood, I could see the leaves of the chestnut trees changing color. It meant that the half-open thistles, showing chestnuts, had already started falling on the ground.

I took a deep breath of the fresh air, and face-palmed with exasperation as I realized that sooner or later, I would have to do it: face my father.

The upcoming events gave me stress and anxiety, fueling the intrusive thoughts inside my head. It made me feel more and more unhappy.

But I had to get all the weight off my chest. After all, I had promised Lucia that I would talk to my father about her.

Suddenly, a knock on the door brought me back from the rumination. Without a whim, I walked to the door and opened it.

It was my mother. "Good morning, Ma," I said, "what's going on?"

She stroked my cheek. "Nothing," she said, "come downstairs, and have breakfast with us."

"Okay, Ma, I'll be right down," I said. "I want to talk to Daddy anyway, before going to church."

I walked downstairs, and I stood in the doorway of the kitchen. My father sat at the table, hands wrapped around a coffee cup, staring at the tablecloth like it could tell him something.

I sat across from him. He didn't look up when I spoke. "Dad…can I talk to you?"

He nodded slightly, still avoiding my eyes. I watch him quietly for a moment, trying to read the man I had grown up with but never truly known.

My father hadn't stepped into a church since the day he married my mother. He didn't believe in confession. Said no man needed a priest to face what he already knew inside. And yet, somehow, he had decided that I should become one.

Maybe it was tradition. Maybe it was pride. Maybe he thought it would fix something in our name that had never been broken.

But I hadn't come to argue theology. I came for one reason. "Dad, there's something I need from you," I said. "Not today. Maybe not even tomorrow. But before your life ends, I want you to recognize her."

He blinked. "Her?"

"Lucia," I said. "She's not just someone I met. She's not a mistake. She's the truth I've found, not the one someone handed me."

He didn't speak. Not right away. Just sat there, coffee growing cold in his hands, as if my words had cracked something deep inside.

"You want me to bless it," he said finally. "What you feel."

"No," I replied. "Not bless it. Just see it. And speak her name out loud. Like she matters."

I glanced at my mother, who had a smile on her face. My father looked at me then, really looked, like he was seeing the boy he'd raised and the man I was becoming, both at once.

"I can't promise much," he said. "But I can promise I'll think about it."

That was enough for now. After I drank my cappuccino, I stepped out into the early morning sunlight. The mountain of Paolisi bathed in a golden hush.

The air from the mountain smelled like damp stone and moss. I didn't feel triumphant. But I didn't feel broken either.

It was something in between—like a door had creaked open inside a house that had always been locked.

After serving Mass, as I always did on Sunday, I returned home, got my bike, and went to visit Lucia at the convent.

The nuns were used to seeing me there often. They knew exactly who I was, and they were happy for Lucia about that.

One of them told me that Lucia was sitting in the garden. She was sitting beneath the fig tree near the convent's back wall, her notebook open, pen resting between her fingers.

She looked up before I even said a word, as if she'd felt me coming.

She turned to me. "Well?" she asked.

I sat beside her, "I told him."

Lucia's face stayed still, but her eyes searched mine. "And?"

"I didn't ask for permission. Just recognition. I told him that before he leaves this life, he has to say your name. Out loud. Not as a sin. As someone who matters."

She stared at me for a long moment, and then quietly closed her notebook.

"Do you think he will?" she asked.

I looked out at the hill, at the sun sinking behind Monte Taburno.

I sighed. "I think he heard me. And that's more than I expected."

Lucia leaned her head against my shoulder. We didn't speak after that. We didn't need to. For that moment, the silence was ours—not his, not the convent's, not the world's. Just ours. `

After saying goodbye, until next month, I rode my bike home. I had school the next day, and I needed to do homework.

I didn't have the luxury to drift. I had already seen what it means to lose your path. Now, I was determined to build, not the one dictated by my father, but a path of my own, with a purpose.

The courses were hard. Calculus, physics, structural mechanics—they pushed me to the edge. But I found a rhythm. I studied at the library most evenings, sometimes until the lights flickered off.

I stopped by cafes only occasionally. I avoided parties, mostly. It wasn't discipline out of pride–it was focus born from necessity.

By the end of the year, the numbers had dropped. Many of the faces from the first lecture hall were gone. But I was still there. And not just hanging on–I had passed into the second year with high grades.

When I saw the results posted, with my name high on the list, I didn't celebrate loudly. I just folded the paper and walked outside, feeling the sun on my face.

I was no longer the boy from the seminary. Not the lost teenager on the riverbank. I was becoming someone new. Someone capable.

Chapter 13

Summer came, and with it, a kind of stillness. I played soccer with my childhood friends under the fading light, their lives seemingly untouched by the confusion that ran just under my skin.

We laughed until our sides hurt. The days stretched long, the evenings filled with dust, grilled bread, and the hum of cicadas.

I visited Lucia once a month. We never said what we felt, not directly. We couldn't. There were too many boundaries spoken and unspoken.

The world called her a distant cousin, but the truth sat between us like a shadow neither of us could step out of: she was my half-sister.

And yet, when I looked at her, I didn't see family the way the world meant it. I saw someone who understood me without translation.

Someone whose presence made the world quieter and more dangerous at the same time.

I tried to meet other girls–in Paolisi, on the train to Benevento, in the cafes near school.

They were kind. They smiled. Some even stirred something like curiosity in me. But none of them reached that place inside me that Lucia already lived in.

Maybe it was guilt. Maybe it was fear. Or maybe it was something else entirely. The fact was that no one seemed right for me.

The two months off from school vanished like breath on a mirror. Long warm days filled with laughter, the exhaustion of soccer matches, and the quiet ache that came every time I left Lucia behind.

I didn't expect answers anymore, just a little peace. Maybe that was enough.

It was Monday, a week before school resumed, when I had to go back to Benevento, just to collect my book list and course information.

I took the early morning train, as I always did–half out of habit, half for the way the light touched the hills at that hour, casting them in gold and green.

The morning felt ordinary. The usual sound–the wheels rattling over the track, the soft murmur of conversation, the rustle of newspapers.

I made my way to the last car of the train. I always preferred it–less crowded, quieter, as if the noise and chatter of the world faded just a little at the back. The routine comforted me.

I slid into a seat by the window and set my school bag on the seat beside me, half hoping it would stay empty, half not caring.

The train just left the station humming to life, and I leaned my head against the glass, watching the walnut trees blur past.

Suddenly, I heard her voice. "Excuse me…is this seat taken?"

I turned, but not fully–not at first. My eyes fell on the edge of her skirt, a pleated plaid that stopped just above the knee.

Her legs were crossed lightly, the posture effortless. Something about the way she stood–the calm, the poise–made the moment slow down.

I lifted my gaze, I took in the rest of her without meaning to: slim, composed, almost too perfectly placed in that train aisle as if she were meant to be there.

Her blouse tucked neatly into the waistband of the skirt, the curve of her shoulders, the confidence in how she held herself.

And then her face. Framed by shoulder–length hair, soft and straight, parted just slightly off–center.

Eyes that met mine without hesitation. A mouth not quite smiling, but full of something kind, something steady.

I froze for an instant. Not out of nerves, but awe. It wasn't just that she was beautiful, though she was.

It was the way everything about her seemed to belong to that exact moment. Like she was part of some quiet order the world had kept hidden until then.

I cleared my throat, shifted my bag without saying much. "No. Please…have a seat."

She sat beside me, and just like that, everything I thought I understood about peace, presence, and desire shifted, quietly but unmistakably.

She settled into the seat, smoothing her skirt gently as the train, which had already made a stop, gave a small lurch forward.

"Do you want to put your school bag on the overhead rack?" I asked her.

"Yes, thank you," she said, handing it to me. So, I got up and placed both of our bags up there.

"I walked through the first two cars," she said, adjusting the strap of her purse. "No empty seats anywhere. Then I got to this car, and I guess I got lucky."

She smiled as she said it. Not a forced smile—an easy one, warm and open, like she was already comfortable here beside me.

I looked at her, letting the corners of my mouth turn up. "It wasn't luck," I said. "I was waiting for you to come."

For a second, she blinked—just a flicker of surprise—and then her smile deepened, touched by something a little more curious, maybe even amused.

She tilted her head slightly, as if trying to decide whether I was serious. The truth was, I hadn't planned the words. They just came.

And somehow, they felt true, not just a line, but something the day itself had conspired to make happen.

The train moved through the countryside. For the first time in a long while, I wasn't thinking about the past or the weight I carried.

Just the girl beside me. Just the way her presence felt like it belonged here, in this seat, next to mine.

It hit me after a few minutes that I hadn't even introduced myself.

"I'm Felice," I said, turning towards her as the train curved gently through the hills.

She smiled again, soft and direct. We shook hands. "Laura."

The name fit her somehow—elegant without being delicate, like it had its own quiet rhythm.

We slipped easily into conversation, the kind that feels like it's already been happening, as if we'd just stepped back into it after a long pause.

She asked, "Do you always take the early train?"

"Every day, once school starts," I said.

"Classes begin next week. This'll be my second year in Benevento."

She nodded. "First for me."

Her voice carried a mix of nerves and excitement, the kind that only comes with something new.

"My father is a teacher. He used to work in Naples, but he just got transferred—finally—to his hometown."

"Oh yeah?" I asked. "Where is that?"

"Where I got on the train. Rotondi," she said casually, like it was another small town.

But something stirred in me. Rotondi. The name hung in the air like a bell still ringing.

That was where Lucia lived. Where I had traced so many secret steps and buried so many unspoken thoughts.

I didn't say anything at first, just let the coincidence settle. It was almost too perfect, too strange.

Laura, this girl who had just sat beside me by chance, if it really was a chance, had unknowingly stepped into the same orbit as my past. And yet, she felt like the beginning of something entirely new.

We kept talking as the train rattled on through the countryside. Conversation came easily, like we'd known each other longer than a few minutes.

No awkward pauses, just the slow unfolding of details. Turned out we were enrolled at the same institute. Not the same program, but close.

"I'm in engineering," I told her. "Second year."

She raised an eyebrow. "Second year? Then we're peers."

"You?"

"Pedagogy," she said. "Also, second year—but my first was in Naples. This is my first time in Benevento. I'm just here today for orientation, to get my book list, see how things work."

I smiled. "Then maybe I can help."

She looked at me, playfully suspicious. "Help?"

"Sure," I said. "When we get there, I can show you where the school is. Whether or not you need my help, I'll be around. And after, if you're not in a hurry…maybe we could have lunch together."

She tilted her head, her long hair brushing one shoulder. "One step at a time," she said, then continued smiling. "Yes–show me where the school is. We can walk there from the station. Once I'm done, I'll think about having lunch with you."

That "I'll think about it" wasn't a brush-off. It was a spark. A challenge. The kind that made the day feel like it had only just begun.

And just like that, the train rolled forward, carrying the two of us into a new chapter I hadn't seen coming.

When the train pulled into Benevento, the platform was already buzzing with students and workers, all pouring into the city for another day of routine.

But for Laura and me, it wasn't routine, not yet. It was a beginning, wrapped in that quiet energy of something not yet defined.

We left the station side by side, walking towards the institute. The city felt warm, familiar to me by then, but I saw it differently that morning, with Laura beside me, pointing out old buildings, asking questions, laughing softly when I explained how confusing the city streets could be.

As we approached the institute, we reached a point where we had to split, her department in one direction, mine in the other.

The Calore River was just a block away, glinting through the narrow line of buildings and traffic. You could see it from the steps of the school, separated only by a busy avenue.

The small bridge, just for pedestrians, stretched across it like a quiet thread tying the old part of the city to the new.

I'd crossed it a hundred times before, but that day, it meant something more.

Before we parted, I turned to her. "Let's meet after," I said. "Whoever finishes first–wait on the bridge, there are benches there."

She nodded. "Deal."

She smiled again, and this time it stayed with me as she turned and walked towards her building.

I stood there for a moment, watching her go, the sound of the city rising around me.

Somehow, just knowing she'd be waiting, or that I'd be waiting for her, made the whole day feel lighter.

I finished before she did, as I expected. Her being new meant more steps, more questions, more paperwork to fill out. I didn't mind.

I walked to the bridge and sat on one of the benches overlooking the Calore. The river shimmered beneath the late morning sun, cars rumbling behind me on the avenue.

My school bag sat beside me, untouched. I watched the street, my eyes drifting to the school entrance now and then, searching.

Almost forty-five minutes passed. Then I saw her. I glanced at my watch; it was 11:30, the perfect time, if she agreed, to stop somewhere for lunch, if…

She stepped out onto the sidewalk, adjusting the strap over her shoulder. Her eyes scanned the avenue, then settled in the direction of the bridge.

She saw me at the same time I saw her. But she was across the street, separated from me by the chaos of traffic–buses, mopeds, the endless rhythm of a city going about its business.

We stood on opposite sides, waiting for the walk signal to turn green. And in that small, suspended moment, something new inside me took place.

She stood there in the light breeze, her skirt moving just slightly, hair brushing against her cheek. Calm, graceful, unhurried.

She wasn't smiling–yet–but there was something in the way she looked at me across the street. Not surprised. As she had known I'd be right there, waiting.

I couldn't help. I was falling for her. Not like I did before. Not with confusion or guilt. This was something else–quiet, clear, certain.

She was, without question, the most beautiful girl I had ever seen.

The light finally changed. She stepped off the curb, weaving through the crowd, her eyes never quite leaving mine.

When she reached me, there was a small pause–like we both felt something had shifted between us in that stretch of waiting, of watching.

"You waited," she said.

"Of course," I replied. "You said you'd think about lunch. I was hoping you'd say yes, or perhaps you want to catch the 12:30 train and go back home?"

She smiled wider now, no more hesitation in it. "Well," she said, brushing a strand of hair from her face, "I'm hungry."

That was all it took. We crossed back over the bridge, this time side by side, walking slowly through the narrow streets of the old part of the city.

We stopped at a place very familiar to me. I had been there before, more than once, with my friends from school.

A place tucked away from the noise, where time seemed to stretch.

The table was near a window. The smell of fresh bread, basil, and something roasting in the back kitchen filled the air.

We ordered pizza with buffalo mozzarella, fresh basil, and mushrooms. And a bottle of Pellegrino, sparkling water.

While enjoying our food, we talked about school, home, books, and little things. I told her about engineering, how I'd ended up there after the seminary.

She didn't press, but her eyes told me she was curious. She shared stories about Naples, her friends, and her father's pride in finally coming home.

Everything about the conversation was easy. And in that ease, something inside me relaxed, as if I had been holding my breath for too long.

I didn't talk about Lucia. Not yet. And when we did, I realized that the world we live in is so small.

She was from Rotondi, the next town over from Paolisi, practically attached to it. I always had to go there to catch the train, since the two towns shared the station.

As we talked about past relationships, she told me that during her time in Naples, she had never met anyone she really liked. She had never dated seriously.

When I told her about Lucia, she paused. She and Lucia had gone to school together for years before she moved to Naples.

She knew the story that Lucia had entered the convent to become a nun, but she had never known who the boy was. Now she did.

She looked at me with private understanding. "It wasn't your fault. Everyone in town knows exactly what happened, twenty years ago," she said, to my surprise.

By sitting across from Laura, in the soft light of a Benevento afternoon, I started to believe that maybe–just maybe–there was a future I hadn't let myself imagine.

Later, on the train ride home, we sat close, talking quietly while the soft rhythm of the train filled the space between our words.

I told her something I hadn't shared with many people–that I'd kept a very accurate diary ever since I first learned how to write. It was how I made sense of things, how I remembered.

Then I said something even more personal: if there was truly a chance to start something new with her, I would begin a new diary. A blank one. I would put the old memories to sleep, not erase them, but let them rest.

She listened without interruption, and then gave me a smile that said more than words. She seemed moved by mine.

An hour later, we got to Rotondi. Before we parted at the station, we agreed to meet again the next day, Tuesday. We only had until the following Monday before returning to school.

We knew very well that from Monday onward we would travel together, but something had already begun on the very day we met.

Chapter 14

As I started to walk the two kilometers back home, I couldn't get Laura out of my mind. I loved everything about her–the calm voice, the way she listened, the way she looked at me like she could see more than I said.

Something had changed in me, and I think my mother noticed it the moment I walked in the door.

"You seem different," she said, not accusing, just observing.

I smiled. "Ma, I met a beautiful girl this morning on the train."

She paused, then gave me a long, thoughtful look. "Be very careful," she said gently. "You've already been burned once."

She wasn't wrong. The wound from Lucia wasn't fresh, but hadn't fully healed either. Still, something about Laura felt different, not like a replacement, not a way to forget, but maybe a way to move forward.

After dinner, I met up with a few of my friends. We stood in the usual spot, kicking at the gravel, talking about nothing at first.

But I couldn't hold it in for too long, I told them about my encounter with Laura.

I didn't go into every detail, but enough for them to see something had happened.

They all said the same thing my mother had: "Be careful. Don't rush."

But it was already too late for caution. I was about to dive in headfirst, and I knew it.

That night, back in my room, everything felt quieter but fuller–like something had settled into place. I pulled open my desk drawer and took out a brand-new diary, its cover stiff, its pages clean and waiting.

I opened to the first page and began to write notes about the day, trying to capture it before any detail faded.

At the top of the page, without hesitation, I wrote: *"Laura, I lov...."*

I was about to write "I love you," but I stopped short.

I said it again in my head, over and over, as if trying to make sense of the feeling–or give it permission to exist.

I had learned those words when I was very little, from my mother.

A short phrase, simple in form but vast in meaning, depending on when and to whom you say it.

The first time I ever said it was to my mother. The second time, I said it to a girl who later turned out to be my half-sister.

After that, I became afraid of those words. Afraid of what they might mean, where they might lead.

It wasn't for fear of commitment, but I was deeply in touch with my emotions. I wasn't afraid of the idea of a relationship, but I was afraid to say those words again to just anyone.

I thought that if I found someone I really liked, I wanted to make sure she was the right person before saying those words again.

Two years had passed since I became aware of the terrible blunder, and at seventeen I was wondering if love existed for real.

I had seen people in romantic relationships, but I wondered if they really loved each other, or if they were just pretending.

During those two years, I had met other girls, but no one seemed right for me, so during that whole time, I hadn't dated any of them for real.

During my adolescence, I had experienced things that left a scar on me. I had seen my father treat my mother badly.

I had seen him cheating on her with another woman at least once.

The worst one was when I found out that he had impregnated two women at the same time.

I had seen that kind of behavior all the time in real life. I thought that just like my father, there had to be many others who acted the same way.

I knew I needed more time to recover from the shock since it became evident that the two years' time was not enough.

Trusting people, in general, was difficult for me back then, and I was constantly thinking that a genuine connection seemed almost impossible.

But tonight, writing them down felt different. It wasn't reckless. It wasn't a rush. It felt…true.

The next morning came with a quiet, steady anticipation. I woke up early, even though we weren't meeting until noon.

I took my time getting ready—not to impress, but because something about the day felt important, sacred almost.

We had agreed to meet at the villa in Rotondi, the same place where, not so long ago, I used to meet Lucia.

Just thinking of it stirred something inside me—a mix of longing, grief, and something new I wasn't ready to name.

The place held so many memories, and now it was about to hold something else.

I arrived a little early and walked the edges of the courtyard, the same worn path I had paced so many times before.

The stone bench where Lucia once sat in silence, the oak tree whose branches had grown heavier since, even the echo of laughter that still seemed to live in the corners—all of it was still there, but different now. Like a stage waiting for a new scene to begin.

At exactly noon, Laura appeared. She was calm, composed, but her eyes lit up when she saw me. That was enough to tell me she had been looking forward to this too.

We walked slowly through the villa grounds, talking lightly at first. She showed me the school building she once attended, and pointed out a small chapel where she used to sit alone.

The same streets I had walked with the weight of the past were now taking on new color, reshaped by her presence.

At one point, we stopped under a weeping willow. She looked at me and said, "You're not like the boys I met in Naples."

I didn't fully understand what she meant, but I knew how it made me feel.

I smiled. "You're not like anyone I've met."

And just like that, the villa–once a place tied to another story–became something else. Not a replacement. Not a repetition. Just…something new. And real.

After we walked through the villa, we didn't want the day to end. There was something easy about being with Laura–no need to impress, no pressure to fill every silence.

We ended up at a small cafe just off the main piazza in Rotondi. It was quiet, shaded by an old awning, the kind of place where time seemed to slow down

We each ordered a granita–lemon for her, coffee for me. She teased me about mine being too bitter, and I told her hers was too sweet.

We laughed, not just at the flavor, but at how natural it felt to sit across from each other like that, like we'd done it a hundred times before.

She asked me about the seminary life, about the discipline, the structure, the silence. I told her it made me stronger in some ways, but lonelier in others.

I didn't say it directly, but I think she understood that part of what I was learning was not just theology or Latin–but how much I missed connection, warmth, love.

She told me more about Naples–how overwhelming it could be, how sometimes she felt invisible in the crowd.

"There, you're just another face," she said. "But here…I feel seen."

I looked at her and said quietly, "I see you."

She held my gaze for a long moment. Nothing dramatic happened, no sudden confessions, no touching of hands, but it was enough. Something between us was already taking root.

As the afternoon wore on and the shadows grew longer, we walked slowly back towards the villa, not wanting the day to end.

A gentle silence passed between us, filled with the warmth of what had just begun.

Before we parted, she asked, "Will you write about today?"

I smiled. "I already have. In my mind. I'll put it on paper tonight."

Then we talk about when we might see each other again.

"I wish I could see you tomorrow," I said. "But I promised my grandparents, as I do every year, that I'd help with the grape harvest. Starts tomorrow. I sleep there. Four full days– picking, pressing, and preparing the wine."

She nodded with real understanding. "That's important. Family comes first."

I was relieved she didn't seem disappointed. "But Monday," I added, "We'll see each other at the station. School starts again, and after that…we'll be seeing each other every day."

She smiled, and this time it was soft but unmistakably hopeful.

We hugged, gently but fully, and then we split–her toward her house, me toward Paolisi. The road between us had never felt shorter.

That night, I sat down at my desk, opened the new diary, and turned to the second page. The ink was still fresh from yesterday's entry, when I had written, *"Laura, I lo..."*

Now I added:

Tuesday.

I saw her again today. We spent the whole day together—walking, talking, sharing. I felt like something clean and good. Something simple but real. She listened to me. She laughed with me. She looked at me in a way that made me feel known. I told her the truth about the harvest, about how I'd be gone for four days. And she understood. No drama. No testing. Just truth. Before we parted, we hugged. It wasn't a long embrace, but it meant something. It was her saying, "I'm here." It was me saying, "Wait for me."

Monday will come. I'll see her at the station. We'll be in the same rhythm again. But until then, this page holds today, so I can carry it with me while I work the vines.

The next four days were spent in the vineyard behind my grandparents' farmhouse. The work was hard, but familiar—sun on my neck, the sticky scent of crushed grapes in the air, the steady rhythm of picking and pressing.

My hands turned purple with juice, and by the end of each day, I was bone-tired. But somewhere inside, I was alive.

Each night, after the noise of the family faded and the cellar doors were closed, I would sit for a moment alone and think of Laura.

I didn't write—there was no time, and maybe I wanted to save the words for when I could see her again.

I imagine her walking through Rotondi, imagine her smile, the sound of her voice. Monday couldn't come soon enough.

And finally, it did.

I woke early and walked to the station, the cool morning air brushing my face. The sky was barely touching the sun.

The train platform was quiet at first, just a few familiar faces. Then I saw her.

Laura.

She smiled, not shyly, but as if we were picking up a conversation from a few minutes ago instead of five days before.

We sat together in the same compartment. As the train pulled away from the station, our knees touched just slightly, and neither of us moved.

We talked in low tones, careful not to disturb the others. There was nothing big or dramatic in our words, just warmth, comfort, the joy of being near again.

Somewhere between Rotondi and Benevento, the train dipped into a stretch of trees, and in that little hush of light and shadow, I turned to her. She turned too.

No need for permission. We kissed.

It was soft, brief, and yet it seemed to echo in the corners of the train car, even if no one else noticed.

When we pulled apart, we didn't speak right away. We just smiled, quietly. Something had changed–something real had begun.

Chapter 15

After the kiss, the world felt different, gentler, like it had finally fallen into step with what I was feeling inside. We didn't say much after that, just shared quiet glances and the occasional touch of knees or shoulders when the train leaned into a curve.

There was no need for explanation. The kiss had already said everything. We arrived at the school in Benevento, and we parted without ceremony. We were careful.

The world we had just entered, school corridors, teachers, classmates, was not the world we had shared on the train.

But even from a distance, I could feel her presence. She was just down the hall, just across the courtyard.

Our routine had changed, but not our rhythm. We started to find small ways to stay connected: a glance in the hallway, a note tucked into a book, a shared moment by the fountain before heading to class.

It didn't take much. Just knowing she was there made everything feel lighter.

During lunch, we found a quiet spot behind a wall where no one usually went. We sat side by side, not touching, just talking about classes, teachers.

She told me she had never been this happy to be back at school. We kissed before going back into our respective classrooms, looking forward to the bell's ringing.

By the time we caught the train back home, we didn't even have to say it out loud; we sat together again. When the train rumbled into that stretch of trees, our hands found each other, fingers lacing without hesitation, and we kissed.

The ride was short, but I didn't measure time in minutes anymore. I measured it in heartbeats, in glances, in the warmth of her hand in mine.

As the days turned into weeks, a rhythm settled over everything. Morning began with the shared walk to the train station, then the ride to school, our quiet bubble of time.

At school, we kept things discreet. Not because we were hiding anything, but because what we had didn't need to be flaunted.

Still, little signs gave us away. A glance that lingered too long. A laugh that carried across the hallway. The way we always seemed to walk together during lunch break.

And soon, the teasing from some of my classmates began.

"Felice, you've been smiling too much lately. Who's the lucky girl?"

Or from her side: "Laura, I didn't know algebra made people that happy."

We played along, laughed with them. But deep inside, we knew what we were growing together wasn't a joke. It was something real, something slow but steady. It was love that was blooming.

It wasn't the kind of love that demanded to be seen. It was the kind that was content to grow silently.

And at night, when the house was still, I sat at my desk and wrote:

Thursday.

The way she looks at me when I say her name—I don't know how to describe it. It's like something opens inside her, and I can see it, even if she doesn't say a word. I didn't expect this. I thought maybe I was done with love. But now I think it was just waiting for her.

Things between us grew deeper, not louder. There was no need for declaration–we lived in the small things. A saved seat. A shared sandwich under the linden tree behind the school. The kind of intimacy that doesn't shout, but sinks into the skin.

But the world doesn't always stay silent.

One afternoon, as we waited for the train back home, she noticed two boys from her town standing off to the side. One of them nudged the other, nodded towards us, and smirked.

She said she knew them from her neighborhood, older, talkative, the kind who noticed everything and had an opinion about even more.

Later, on the ride home, they sat across from us. Laura leaned close and whispered, "They were watching on the platform, and are still looking at us. One of them is my neighbor."

"I saw," I said. "Let them watch all they want to."

She nodded, but I could tell something in her had stiffened. Not fear exactly, Laura wasn't the fearful kind, but awareness.

That we weren't invisible anymore, that what we had might soon be judged, questioned, or even gossiped about. In our small town, words travel faster than the wind.

The next day, while at school in the hallway, someone made a comment loud enough to hear but not enough to confront: "Looks like Felice found someone to keep him company during breaks."

I ignored it, but Laura pulled back a little that day–still kind, still smiling, but more guarded. I couldn't blame her. She had seen how stories spread before, and not all stories end kindly.

That night, I wrote in my diary:

The days that followed were quieter. Not between us, between the world and us. Laura became more careful, more aware of where we stood, who might be watching.

She still smiled when we met in the hallway. She still found her way to my side on the train. But she didn't reach for my hand like before. She didn't lean quite as close.

And I understood.

For a few days, we drifted slightly, still in each other's orbit, but guarded. It hurt, not because she was distant, but because I knew it wasn't her choice entirely.

It was the way the world was back then that had pushed its way between us. The whispering, the smirks, the assumptions.

Then came Monday morning.

We met on the platform as usual, but something in her had changed again, her eyes softer, her hand brushing mine just before we stepped onto the train. A small gesture, but enough to say: *"I'm still here."*

Halfway through the ride, she turned to me and whispered, "Do you think they'll ever stop talking?"

I thought for a moment and said, "No. But we can stop listening."

She looked at me for a long time. And then, in the middle of that full train car, she smiled the way she used to, without fear, and she kissed me.

That afternoon, we didn't hide. We sat in our usual spot behind the school. She rested her head on my shoulder, and I didn't move.

"I love you," she said.

"I love you too," I responded.

Whatever the world might say, we had made our decision. That night, the diary opened to a new page:

Monday.

She came back to me today-not that she ever left, but I felt her return fully. The outside voices faded, or maybe we stopped giving them power. All I know is that she looked at me and chose us again. And I will keep choosing her, every day, for as long as I'm allowed.

Chapter 16

The pressure from outside never truly stopped. People whispered, eyes lingered, and the weight of judgement hung in the air.

But Laura and I couldn't care less. We had learned to turn a deaf ear to the gossip, and our bond was getting stronger than their words.

We began to skip school occasionally, seeking solace in each other's company. We found a secluded spot by the river—a patch of grass where the rest of the world felt distant.

There, amidst nature's embrace, we shared picnics, dreams, and moments of quiet reflection. We had already done it twice, and it felt like a discovery.

One day, even though we knew it was wrong, we did it again; we skipped school. It was the third time we did it, but this time it was different.

The first two times had been innocent enough—at least by the standards of two teenagers hungry for time alone.

So, we went to the same secluded spot near the river. Laura wore a beautiful dress that day—light, soft, flowing just past her knees.

The sun was bright that morning, too warm to waste in a classroom. We took the long path out of the city, down past the old road and towards the river, where we'd found a quiet spot under a tall oak tree.

The grass was soft and wild, the breeze gentle, the world completely ours.

We lay on our plaid blanket, the same one she had brought on our last picnic, and stretched out side by side.

Laura's head rested near my shoulder. We shared some bread, some grapes. We talked, laughed, and held hands. It felt perfect.

I had every intention, if she allowed, to cross that threshold with her. My heart was racing, not with lust alone, but with something more complicated; desire, yes, but also fear, and history.

When the moment came, she didn't pull away. She didn't try to stop me.

She just looked into my eyes. There was trust there. Not pressure. No expectation. Just...openness.

"It will be my first time," she simply said. "I have never been with anyone."

"I know, you told me once before. That makes two of us," I said, as we continued in the act.

Suddenly, something stopped me.

Maybe it was the silence of the trees, or the softness of her breath. Maybe it was the ghost of my father, hovering somewhere in the back of my mind.

A man who never stopped taking what he wanted. A man whose choices had marked my life and the life of the girl I once almost loved, without knowing we shared his blood.

I didn't want to be like him. So I pulled back.

She looked at me–calm, not angry. Not confused, not exactly. But I didn't know what she was feeling. I only knew what I had to say.

"I'm sorry," I whispered.

She touched my hand and said, "It's okay. We don't have to. It's good that you stopped, because we were about to make a big mistake."

She said those words so gently that it almost broke me. I didn't know if she was disappointed or relieved. Maybe both.

But she stayed close. We stayed there in the grass a little longer, listening to the wind move through the leaves, the river running just beyond the reeds.

That night, I wrote in my diary:

Monday.

We could have done it today. She would have let me. But something in me said, "Not yet. Not like this."

I couldn't go through with it-not out of fear of love, but fear of repeating what I've spent my life trying to unlearn.

I don't know if she understands, not completely. But she didn't get upset. She didn't judge. And that means everything.

The next few days passed with a quiet kind of awareness between us.

No tension—more like a thread pulled tighter, humming with things left unspoken. We still sat together on the train.

We still laughed at the same things, still brushed hands when no one was looking. But underneath the familiar gesture, something had changed.

I wasn't sure if she saw me differently now. If my hesitation had hurt her pride or made her feel unwanted. But she didn't seem colder. Just quieter. Thoughtful.

Maybe she was wondering about me the same way I was wondering about her.

One afternoon, after school, we walked a little slower than usual towards the station. We didn't talk much.

Then, just as we reached the platform, she turned to me and said softly, "You don't have to explain."

I looked at her for a moment, and something in her face told me–she did understand. Or at least, she was trying to. And maybe that was enough.

I wanted to say something meaningful, something honest. So I told her, "Laura, look at me. I want you to know that I didn't stop because I didn't want you. I stopped because I didn't want to carry something into our love that didn't belong there."

She looked down, then back up at me. "I know," she said. And just like that, the silence lifted.

We sat together on the train home like we always did, but this time there was no second-guessing. Her head rested on my shoulder again, and I placed my hand over hers. She squeezed back.

That night, I opened my diary with a steady hand.

Friday.

There's a kind of love that doesn't need proving. That day by the river taught me more than anything I'd ever learned in school. Love isn't about what you take, or even what you give—sometimes, it's what you choose to hold back, what you protect.

I don't know where we're going, but I know this: I didn't lose her that day. I think I gained something much more.

We didn't speak of that day by the river again—not directly. But we didn't need to. It lived between us, quietly, like a book set gently on a shelf, waiting to be opened again when the time was right.

And then, one warm October afternoon, we returned.

School had let out early. We had made no plans, but when she looked at me and said, "Do you want to go back?" I knew exactly what she meant.

We walked the long, familiar path without speaking much. The air smelled like dry grass and the last figs on the trees. The world felt suspended, like it was holding its breath just for us.

When we reached the river, our spot looked unchanged–the oak tree overhead, the plaid blanket still folded in my bag like it had been waiting all along.

We spread it out and lay there in the quiet. The sun filtered through the leaves, casting dappled light across her face. She looked over at me and smiled.

This time, when I touched her cheek and leaned closer, she didn't just allow it–she welcomed it.

We shared so many quiet words in that moment–words I've never forgotten. Promises we couldn't possibly keep, and confessions that felt like prayers.

There was no rush. Every movement was deliberate, tender. There was hesitation, yes–but not from fear. From awe. Like we both understood this was something we could never take back, and neither of us wanted to.

I reached under her dress, touched the fabric of her underwear, and gently slipped them down. She closed her eyes. I kissed her neck, her shoulders, her lips, over and over.

What happened next wasn't perfect–it was clumsy, tender, urgent. But it was real. We gave ourselves to each other with innocence, trembling courage, and a longing that had been building for weeks, months.

It wasn't about lust. It was about belonging, about finally expressing with our bodies what we had already said with our hearts.

In that serene setting, we made love for the first time. It was a culmination of our emotions–a blend of affection, curiosity, and youthful passion.

Afterwards, we lay in silence. Her head rested on my chest. I could feel the river flowing nearby, and her breath against my skin. The world kept turning–but we had stopped time, just for a little while.

That night, I poured my thoughts into my diary, capturing every sensation, every emotion.

It was a moment I wanted to preserve, to remember not just the act, but the profound connection we shared.

That night, I didn't even need to think about what to write. The words came like breath;

Monday.

This day will live with me forever. Not because we finally crossed a line, but because of how we crossed it. With care. With love. With eyes wide open.

Laura gave herself to me without fear, and I gave myself to her without shame. This wasn't about desire alone–it was about trust, about letting go of every doubt and holding on to each other instead.

If I live to be a hundred, I will remember the way she looked at me under the oak tree. The way the sun touched her hair. The way, for the first time in my life, I felt completely chosen.

After that day, something between us became both stronger and more fragile. We had crossed a line, yes–but not in shame.

We had stepped into a deeper intimacy, into something that felt real and lasting. But with it came a heightened awareness of everything around us.

Every glance, every word from a teacher, every shift in tone from our parents felt loaded with suspicion, even when it wasn't.

We still saw each other every day, and still went by the river, only occasionally. Skipping school eventually would have impacted our grades, and to avoid compromising future opportunities, we stopped.

We found other places and other ways to be intimate. The pleasure was there, every time, but now it lived side by side with a quiet fear. We were careful, sometimes overly so.

Our love had become a secret we had to protect, even though it deserved to be lived out loud.

I could tell Laura felt it too. She still smiled, still joked with me, still held my hand when no one was watching–but I could sense the worry behind her eyes.

We both knew that people talk, and that in our towns, talk could quickly turn into condemnation. Especially for her, who was afraid of her family finding out about our relationship.

At night, I continued to write. I tried to make sense of what we were feeling, what we were risking.

But I also wrote about the tenderness of her voice, the way the world seemed to pause when we were together.

I was eighteen by then, and that was everything. I didn't know what the future held, but I knew I loved her, at least I thought I did.

Our relationship had lasted almost two years by then. We had fallen into a rhythm–school, secret meetings, letters passed in silence, walks to the river, moments stolen from time.

It felt like a world we had built for just the two of us, and it felt like we could go on together until the end of time. But nothing stays untouched forever in this world. Trouble was quietly building on the horizon.

Chapter 17

Sunday, August 13, 1967. I will never forget that day.

I woke up to the sound of rain hammering against the tiled roof, the kind of rain that doesn't fall gently, but arrives in sweeping gusts like waves against the side of a ship.

The windows rattled softly in their frames, and the air in my room was heavy, like the storm outside had crept into the house.

I was days away from turning nineteen. Summer was fading, it was slipping through my fingers, and with it, a sense of safety we had come to take for granted.

In just a few weeks, I'd be starting my fourth year of school, back to long train rides, back to early mornings and late nights filled with study–and Laura.

But that morning, something else filled the house. A different kind of weather.

From my room, through the door left slightly ajar, from the kitchen, I heard my parents talking in low voices.

At first, I didn't listen. My mind was still drifting in half-sleep, thinking maybe we'd stay inside all day. Maybe I'd write in my diary. Maybe I'd see Laura if the rain let up.

Then I caught one word. One sharp, clear word: *"America."*

I sat up.

That's when I first heard the familiar tension in my father's voice–the same restless tone I had come to associate with changes, with packing, with leaving.

Their voices rose and fell–my father's, steady but serious; my mother's, more anxious, the edge of worry under each phrase.

They were talking about the possibility of leaving. Emigrating. Starting over in the United States.

Despite what I saw as two failed emigrations–Argentina and Australia–my father hadn't given up. He was chasing a third dream. A third escape.

It wasn't the first time I'd heard it mentioned, but it was the first time it felt real.

This time, my father had found his reason: my mother's birth in New York made her an American citizen.

That meant we had a claim. A way in. A new future. A fresh start. But to me, it felt like a goodbye I wasn't ready to face.

Autumn 1967 brought a subtle shift in the air, not just the cool breeze sweeping through Paolisi, but something stirring in my father's voice, his movements, his silence.

A wave passed through me–cold and fast. Suddenly, the room felt unfamiliar, the rain outside more urgent, like a warning.

My whole life, everything I knew–my school, my friends, my future with Laura–it all felt like it was being swept up by the storm.

I didn't move. I just stood there, staring at the tiled floor, listening to the muffled voices from the kitchen, trying to understand what this would mean.

"Why emigrate?" I asked myself, "For what reason?"

The vineyards had been generous that year, the olive trees full, the cellar humming with barrels of new wine. Yet none of it seemed to anchor him. Once again, his thoughts drifted westward–across the sea, to America.

I'd seen it before; his restlessness came in waves. He had spoken of emigration for years, ever since I was small.

Like so many men in the south, he believed the New World held something Italy could no longer promise: prosperity, dignity, a future free of struggle. But until now, it had always remained a dream deferred.

That Sunday morning remains etched in my memory like the first chill of autumn–quiet, still, and filled with the weight of something unspoken shifting in the house.

My father's voice was steady, measured. He spoke of *documenti, richieste* e *passaporti*–words that, until then, had lived more dreams than reality.

And my mother, who had always listened more than spoken when emigration came up, was now asking questions, considering timelines.

She mentioned her cousins in America, the ones in New Jersey, or the ones in the Bronx and Brooklyn, and how they could help–*Ci danno una mano.*[*]

The idea wasn't distant anymore. It had weight. Maybe after the Christmas holidays, my father said. After the new year.

I laid back on my bed, stared at the ceiling, covered my ears with both hands, trying not to listen anymore to something that for me didn't make sense at all.

Although, soon I realized that this time, the dream of America was knocking on our door, stepping into the hallway, packing its bags.

I remember lying there, uncertain of what I felt–torn between curiosity and dread. Part of me wondered what might lie on the other side of the ocean, but another part held tightly to the streets of Paolisi, to Laura, to everything familiar, to everything I wasn't ready to leave behind.

I didn't want to wait for the end of the day to write in my diary, as I usually did. That same morning, I wrote quietly, my hands almost trembling.

---

[*] They'll give us a hand

The rain gradually stopped falling, the sky, though, was still the color of ash, and the street ran with rivers of mud and rainwater coming down from the nearby mountain.

Inside the house, the conversation had ended, but the air was thick with its memory. I went down to the kitchen.

My parents moved about quietly, avoiding my eyes. As if they knew I had heard. As if they weren't ready to answer the questions, they hadn't yet asked me directly.

I couldn't keep still. In the kitchen, I hovered near the window, pretending to be interested in the rain.

My mother approached me, wiping her hands on a towel. I turned to her. "Is it true?" I asked. "Are we really going to America?"

She didn't answer right away. She looked past me, out at the street, then said gently, "Your father's just looking into things. It's only a thought, Felice."

"A thought," I repeated, though I could already feel the ground shifting.

"We're thinking of your future. There are more possibilities there. A better life."

"Ma, yes, it may be a better life. But not this life," I said.

I didn't say anything more. After breakfast, I went back to my room and stared at the ceiling until the rain stopped.

In my chest, a quiet panic had begun to grow. It wasn't just about leaving. It was about everything I would be forced to leave behind.

That evening, I met Laura in Rotondi, at the villa–a routine we had made a habit of. We sat there on the stone bench, just talking, watching couples go by pushing their baby carriage.

I wanted to tell her right then. I almost did. The words reached my lips…and stopped. I didn't want to see her eyes change. Not yet. Not on a day like that.

Instead, I said something about the storm. She smiled and said she had thought about me all morning. I nodded and held her hand a little tighter than usual.

That night, the diary entry came slow but clear:

Sunday, continued.

I asked my mother today. She didn't deny it. It's real. Maybe not now, maybe not soon–but real. And I couldn't tell Laura. I didn't have the courage. Not yet.

What if it ruins what little time we have left? What if it breaks her heart–and mine? The rain stopped, but inside me, it hasn't.

Chapter 18

It was the end of August now, a few days before turning nineteen. Even at that age it didn't mean I was independent—not in Paolisi, not in my family. I listened. That's what sons did. I could have dreamed of staying behind, but the truth was, I had no real say.

How could I remain in my town alone, even if I wanted to? I didn't have the means, the authority, or the courage to go against my father's will.

And Laura? My God—I didn't want to think about telling her. The thoughts of seeing her face, of trying to explain something I could barely accept myself, filled me with a kind of dread I couldn't name.

She was part of the world I was still building, still hoping for. And now the fragile world was at risk of being pulled out from under my feet before it had even taken shape.

It was too soon for me to speak, too soon to decide. So I stayed silent, waiting, listening—watching the days close in around me.

Well, it wasn't official yet—no papers signed, no dates confirmed—I decided, and my parents agreed, to go ahead and enroll in my fourth year of school anyway.

Since it was still only talk—just my parents speaking cautiously about possibilities—I didn't want to scare Laura. Not yet. Not until I knew something for sure.

When we met at the station to go to Benevento and enroll for the new school year, to get the book list and begin another chapter as we always had, I decided to tell her—not as a certainty, but as something that might happen.

We were walking from the station towards the school, when I decided to talk about that subject. The early morning sun glinting off the cobblestone, and the city was alive around us, but for a moment, it felt like we were the only two people in it.

She took my hand, "What are you thinking about?" she said. "It seems like you're not here."

I cleared my throat. "You're right, I'm sorry. There's something I didn't really want to tell you, but I have to, and I don't know how to start."

She stopped, faced me, and raised her eyebrows. "Is it about us? Perhaps a change of mind?"

My eyes filled with tears. "No, how can you even think such a thing?"

She pulled me to the side. "You're crying, so it must be something serious. Go on, tell me, we don't keep secrets from each other."

I stroked her face and started to walk. "I don't want to scare you," I said, careful with my tone.

She glanced at me, her smile fading slightly. "What is it?"

"It's nothing for sure yet, but...." I hesitated. "My parents have started talking again about America. Emigrating. Maybe after Christmas."

She stopped walking again, just for a second, though. "Are you serious?"

"I didn't want to say anything because it's just talk. My mother has cousins there, and my father...well, you know, I told you how he's always been."

Laura looked ahead, as if trying to see what this might mean. Then she turned back at me. "But would you really go? Would they take you?"

"If they go, I go," I said. "I can't stay here alone. I'm not even nineteen."

She nodded slowly. "And what about school? About us?"

"I don't know," I said. "That's why I'm telling you now. Because if it becomes real…we have to know what we are dealing with."

There was silence between us for a moment, the kind that doesn't need to be filled.

She squeezed my hand tightly. "Well," she said finally, her voice steady, "until then, we go on. Right?"

"Of course," I said. And we walked on, each step echoing with questions neither of us could yet answer.

We walked the rest of the way in near silence—not cold or distant, just thoughtful. It was the kind of silence that comes when two people are trying not to break something fragile between them.

Laura held her book close to her chest; I kept glancing at her, wondering what she was really thinking, whether she was already preparing herself for goodbye.

But once we reached the school, something changed. We stepped into the familiar rhythm of enrollment: signing our names, checking the new schedule, collecting the list of books we'd need.

The corridor still smelled of chalk and worn wood, just like every September. Teachers passed by, nodding to returning students, and for a little while, the world felt solid again.

After we finished at school, there was no need to rush back home. We sat at the usual cafe, and as we always did, two cappuccinos.

While waiting for our drinks, she turned to me. "Just a minute," she said. "I'll be right back."

She walked to the counter, and a few minutes later, she came back with a dish with two pastries.

"For your almost-birthday," she said with a smile.

"Thank you," I said. "Why did you go to the counter to get them?" I asked.

"Because I didn't want you to pay for them," she added.

The conversation drifted back to normal things: new subjects, the professor we both hoped wouldn't return, books that cost too much.

"I'm not going to think about America unless it becomes real," Laura said suddenly, breaking the calm. "You shouldn't either."

I know," I replied. "But it's there now. Like a shadow."

She reached across the table and touched my hand lightly. "Then let's stay in the light while we can."

That small moment–her hand, her voice, the steam rising between us–was enough to carry me through the rest of the day.

We gathered our stuff, and without needing to say much, we drifted toward our usual spot by the river–a hidden place just outside the edge of the city, where the trees bent low over the water and the world felt far away.

We had been there before, but that day was different. There was something in the air, in our touch, in the way we looked at each other–more urgent, more tender, more present than ever.

There was no fear, no hesitation–only the need to hold on, to make the moment last, to say with our bodies what we couldn't quite put into words: that we were here, together, now.

And whatever the future might bring–America, distance, change–we had this. That day, by the river, time stopped for us.

We lay there for a while holding hands. I glanced at my watch. "I would like to stay a little longer," I said, "but we don't want to miss the last train."

She jumped up. "Oh my God, I didn't realize how late it is," she said. "Let's go. My parents will kill me if I miss the train."

We started walking back towards the station at a brisk pace. We were both thoughtful; America was still there in our heads.

The streets in Benevento that day seemed unchanged, as if they had no interest in our private fears.

The narrow alleys were full of voices, Vespas zipped past in bursts of sound, and shopkeepers called out their greetings as if nothing in the world could move.

The scent of fresh bread from the forno on Via Napoli, the soft clang of the church bell near Piazza Risorgimento–it was all so reassuring, so rooted.

But beneath every step I took, I felt a quiet unease. Not panic, not sadness–just the knowledge that the world I loved might be temporary.

Every street corner I had memorized, every rhythm of life I had trusted, might soon become memory. And yet, I held tight to that day. To Laura's hand brushing mine. To the thick pages of our new textbook. To the echo of our laughter, even with uncertainty between us.

That day, when we got back to Rotondi, when we split to take our own way home, we didn't say goodbye.

We said, *"See you tomorrow."* And we meant it.

I walked home from the station, and as I walked in, the house smelled of tomato sauce and basil–simple, comforting. I watched my mother working by the stove, her hands moving as always between pots and ladles, her rhythm steady, familiar.

"E' andato tutto bene con l'iscrizione? Hai preso I libri?"* she asked, glancing over her shoulders.

"Si mamma, tutto a posto,"* I said, as I kissed her on both cheeks. I didn't mention anything more. Just, "tutto a posto."

My father was already home, sitting in his usual spot near the window. He glanced up as I walked over to hug him, not suspicious–just curious.

"Ci hai messo tutta la giornata?"* he asked, raising an eyebrow.

---

* "Did everything go well with the registration? Did you get the books?"
* "Yes, Mom, everything's fine."
* "Did it take you the whole day?"

"I was with friends," I said, trying to sound casual.

He smirked. "Yeah, friends. You mean Laura."

I couldn't help smiling. "Okay, Daddy, you got me. I'm in love with her."

He chuckled, clearly enjoying himself. I hesitated a moment, then asked, "Can I ask you something… personal?"

He looked over, a bit amused. "Vai."

"Did you ever date Chiara Milucci when you were young?"

He frowned. "Chiara who?"

"Laura's mother."

He looked puzzled. "Why do you ask that?"

Then he burst out laughing. He turned to my mother and said, "Ma tu lo senti tuo figlio? Hai sentita cosa mi ha domandato?"*

My mother laughed too, shaking her head.

"No, Felice," my father said, still grinning. "I never dated any Chiara Milucci. You're safe."

It turned into a shared laugh, the kind that softened the edges of everything else. For a moment, all the talk of emigration and uncertainty faded into the background.

That night, when I sat down at my desk and opened my diary, I still had a smile on my face.

The air in the house, for once, felt full of warmth instead of uncertainty.

As I wrote in my diary, the moment still lingered. Even with all the unknowns ahead, something in me felt a little more sure of where I stood–and who I loved.

---

* "Do you hear your son? Did you hear what he asked me?"

Oggi e' stato un giorno pieno, in ogni senso.

Sono andato a Benevento con Laura per iscrivermi a scuola e prendere le lista dei libri. Il tempo era ancora estivo, il sole gentile, e il nostro passo tranquillo, come se volessimo rallentare il tempo.

Non abbiamo dovuto marinare la scuola-non era ancora iniziata-cosi', dopo tutto, ci siamo concessi un po' di tempo per noi. Siamo tornati al nostro posto, quello vicino al fiume. Non ci siamo parlati tanto. Non serviva. C'era qualcosa di eterno in quel momento. Anche se so che nulla dura per sempre.

Tornato a casa, mio padre mi ha chiesto perche' ci ho impiegato tanto tempo. Gli ho detto che ero stato con amici. Ha riso:" Si, amici, Laura vuoi dire." Li mi sono arreso: Okay, papa' mi hai beccato. Sono innamorato di lei.

Poi, come uno scemo, gli ho chiesto se conosceva Chiara Milucci-la madre di Laura-per assicurarmi che non stessi frequentando un'altra sorellastra, come mi era capitato pochi anni prima con Lucia. E' scoppiato a ridere, come se fosse un gioco. Anche mia madre. E io pure.

Per un attimo eravamo solo una famiglia che rideva. Senza America, senza incertezza, senza pensare a cose brutte.

E io? Io ero solamente il ragazzo che amava una ragazza, e che sperava, in quel momento, che il domani non sarebbe mai arrivato. *

---

* Today was a full day, in every sense. I went to Benevento with Laura to enroll in school and pick up the book list. The weather was still summery, the sun gentle, and our steps unhurried, as if we were trying to slow time itself.

We didn't have to skip school—it hadn't started yet—so in the end, we stole a little time for ourselves. We returned to our spot, the one by the river. We didn't talk much. There was no need. Something about that moment felt eternal. Even though I know nothing lasts forever.

Back home, my dad asked why it took me so long. I told him I was with friends. He laughed: "Yeah, 'friends'—Laura, you mean." I surrendered: "Okay, Dad, you got me. I'm in love with her."

Then, like an idiot, I asked if he knew Chiara Milucci—Laura's mother—just to make sure I wasn't dating another secret half-sister, like what happened years ago with Lucia. He burst out laughing, as if it were a game. So did my mom. And so did I.

For a moment, we were just a family laughing. No America, no uncertainty, no dark thoughts.

And me? I was just a boy who loved a girl, hoping—right then—that tomorrow would never come.

September came with cooler air and the start of our final school year. Everything should've felt familiar–the train rides, the classrooms, the teachers calling roll. And Laura, always beside me.

But nothing was the same.

We tried, for a while, to keep things light. We studied. We laughed. We sat close on the train. But we both knew the clock had started ticking.

And when I told her the decision was real–when my parents had set the date for January 8–something changed in her. No bitterness. No distance. Just reality.

"I can't come with you, not now, of course, or later if you decide to remain there," she said one afternoon as we sat outside the school, our books between us like a barrier. "You know that," she added.

I nodded. "I know," I said. And I did.

She was an only child. Her parents were older, fragile in ways that didn't always show on the surface but weighed on her.

She couldn't just leave them behind, and she wouldn't. That was part of what I admired about her–her loyalty, her heart. Even when it meant I would lose her.

So we started living in the space between the now and the not-much-longer. We loved each other fiercely, almost desperately.

We still stole time. We still escaped to the river when we could. We still wrote notes and kissed like we could stop time.

But January hovered over us like a second winter.

One evening in late November, after I got home from school, my father called me into the kitchen. The paperwork had been finalized. Passports were in motion. Tickets booked. It's official: *January 8, 1968.*

But there was always hope that once we arrived in New York, my father would have changed his mind, like he did with the two previous emigrations.

Anyway, I went to my room. I sat down, opened my diary, and wrote.

November.

It's no longer a possibility. It's a date. My departure has a date, a month, a fixed point on the horizon. Laura says she understands, but I see the sorrow in her smile.

I don't know how to say goodbye to someone who's still beside me. I don't want this to be our last week. I want to freeze time. But instead, I'll write. Every day until I go. So that something of us will remain.

The weeks that followed were like living in slow motion. Every morning on the train, I held her hand a little tighter.

Every lunch shared, every walk after school, every secret smile across the school hallway—they all felt wrapped in a kind of gold sadness.

We didn't speak often about January. I didn't need repeating. We both knew what was coming.

But we made a quiet decision—maybe not out loud—to love whatever time we had left.

Chapter 19

During those two years, I never forgot about Lucia—my half-sister, still living behind the convent walls. Even as my life moved forward, month by month, I made time to visit her, at times taking my sister Antonietta with me.

It became almost like a quiet ritual: once a month, always on a Sunday, after Mass and after lunch, I'd find a way to go. We didn't have long visits, and we didn't always talk about deep things.

Sometimes we just sat in the garden or in the small visiting parlor, and she'd ask how school was going or how my parents were. But little by little, we opened up more.

One day, I brought up Laura—not to confess anything, just out of curiosity.

"She told me you two went to school together," I said.

Lucia smiled, a little surprised. "Yes, for a few years. She was in my class when we were younger. She was always quiet. Kind. The teacher liked her."

There was no jealousy in her tone, no awkwardness. Just good memories.

It struck me then how small our world really was, and how strangely connected all our paths had become—mine, Laura's, Lucia's.

As if life had been weaving us together long before we understood what it meant.

There wasn't much free time during the week, just weekends, which always felt short. For a while, it felt like we had found a balance. Life wasn't perfect, but it was ours.

Then December came–and with it: No more "maybe." No more "we'll see after the holidays." It was happening. The date of our departure was set, January 8, 1968, after spending the holidays with the grandparents.

This time we weren't crossing the ocean on a ship, but on an airplane. Alitalia Airlines.

"But there's a thread of hope," I said to Laura one day, needing to give her something, anything. "If I know my father…we won't last long over there. We'll be back."

She looked at me for a long moment, then gave a small nod. I don't know if she believed me. I don't even know if I believed myself.

But saying it gave us something to hold on to, something that felt like a promise, even if it wasn't one I could truly make.

She didn't answer right away. We kept walking in silence for a few steps, the gravel crunching under our shoes. Then she stopped, turned to me, and spoke softly.

"So you're really going," she said–not as a question, but as something she was trying to accept out loud.

I nodded. "Yes. But not forever. I swear. My father–he has a history of giving up on things quickly. If it doesn't go as he dreams, we'll be back."

She gave me a faint smile, but it didn't quite reach her eyes, "You say that now," she said. "But America isn't the next town over. It's a different world. And once you leave…" She looked down. "Everything changes."

"I don't want anything to change," I whispered. "Not us."

She looked up again, steady now, even if her voice was thin. "Then don't let it. Wherever you go, don't forget who we are. What we've been. What we are.",

I reached for her hand. "I couldn't forget you if I tried."

She held my hand tightly, as if to memorize its shape. Then, almost to herself, she said, "If you leave, you have to promise me something."

"Anything."

"You write to me. Often. Like I'm still there with you."

"I will."

"Even if I don't write back sometimes. You keep writing."

"I will."

And we just stood there, not holding on to time–just each other. "Just three weeks left," she said.

All I could do was nod.

Christmas lights began to appear in windows and along the main street. People talked about the *Cenone,* about midnight Mass, about New Year's fireworks.

But for Laura and me, the season felt different. Everything was heavier. Bright on the surface, but darker underneath.

We didn't talk much about the departure. Not directly. It hung between us like fog–always there, always waiting.

We tried to make those weeks feel normal. We went to school. We studied. We exchanged gifts–small, simple things with too much meaning.

Sometimes we'd smile and pretend nothing was changing. Other times, we held each other like it was the last time.

The hardest part was the silence around us–how we couldn't tell our friends, how we kept it just between us. I don't know if that made it more real or less. But those weeks, every moment felt like it mattered more than it should.

A look, a word, a walk after school–all of it became a memory before it even finished happening. And still, the day kept moving. Christmas came. The New Year's. And then only a handful of days remained.

Chapter 20

It was Sunday, January 7th, 1968–the day before we were to leave for America. The worst day of my life, when I had to say goodbye to everything that was so precious to me, that I was living behind.

The air was still, and the town quiet after the holidays. Decoration sagged in windows, the last panettone crumbs lingered on kitchen tables, and church bells rang with a tired rhythm.

I spent the earlier part of the morning in church, as usual. I served the Mass for the last time and said goodbye to the archpriest.

When I got home, I asked my father if I could take the car for an hour or two.

"To go where?" he asked.

"To do my duty," I said, in a sad way. "I have to say goodbye to Lucia before I leave. You forgot about her?" I asked.

He didn't answer. He glanced at me sideways, reaching inside his jacket pocket. "Here're the keys," he said.

I took them from his hand, then I walked into the kitchen and told my mother I was going to the convent.

I didn't go alone. I brought my eighteen-year-old sister Antonietta with me–it was only the third time she had ever seen Lucia.

Lucia greeted us in the small visiting room. She smiled when she saw Antonietta and leaned closer, her voice warm.

"She looks like you," she said, then turned to me, her expression softening.

"I don't just look like him, you look like us," said Antonietta, smiling.

I cleared my throat. "Antonietta, Lucia is aware of that."

We spoke for a little while–about school, about the holidays, about nothing important. I kept glancing at her, trying to memorize the details of her face.

Finally, I told her. "We came to say goodbye. We're leaving in the morning," I said. "For America."

Lucia nodded slowly, as if she had expected it.

Then I tried, carefully, to open a door. "Lucia, maybe…one day you could come too. Not now, of course. But eventually. You are family, and with the proper paperwork, you'll be allowed to come. I could take care of it once we have established. What do you say?"

Her expression didn't change. She lowered her eyes for a moment, then looked at me with a kind of calm finality. "What can I say? I'm not going anywhere, Felice," she responded.

"I've decided. I'm staying, my life is here. I'm going to take my vows. This…this will be my life. I have made peace with it," she said without fear, without regrets.

I looked at her for a long moment, searching for sadness in her eyes, but there was none. Just calm. Acceptance. Maybe even joy.

I nodded. "I understand, Lucia."

We didn't need to say more. We said goodbye with a quiet understanding between us.

There were no tears, just the press of hands, and the weight of what words couldn't carry.

And in that moment, I saw the full distance between where we had been and who we had become.

Lucia was no longer the girl I met at the theater, wide–eyed and curious. She was committed, steady, rooted in something I could no longer touch.

When we walked away, Antonietta was unusually quiet. I didn't ask her what she was thinking. Some moments are better left untouched.

And as we stepped back into the winter light, I knew: whatever waited for me across the ocean, a piece of my heart would always remain behind those convent walls.

That evening, after returning from the convent, the sky turned pale and heavy. By dinnertime, snow had begun to fall—light at first, then steadier, covering the rooftops and narrow street in a soft white hush.

I went out one last time, walking through town alone. The lights from the windows glowed golden against the snow.

I passed the church, the bar, the social club—every place that had shaped my life in ways I hadn't yet fully understood.

I didn't go see Laura that night. We had already said goodbye in our way, in the days before. This was a quieter farewell, between me and the town itself.

Inside the house, suitcases stood by the door. My mother moved through the kitchen in silence, checking and rechecking everything.

My father paced more than usual, smoking by the window. My siblings sat at the table, drawing something on scraps of paper. None of us said much.

Later that evening, I wrote in my diary:

Sunday. January 7, 1968.

I saw Lucia early today. Maybe for the last time. I asked her if she'd ever come to America, just to plan the thought. She said no. Her heart is set.

She's chosen a different life. And for the first time, I felt no pull, no confusion. Just respect. And closure. That chapter is not closed yet. She remains part of my family, part of my life.

I went to bed after that. I tried, but I couldn't sleep. And when morning came, the snow was still falling.

It was January 8th, 1968.

Before sunrise, the van came to pick us up, and we began the long ride to Rome airport. The road out of town was quiet, the snow muffling every sound.

I looked out the window as we passed the old school, the church, the square, the hills I had known all my life. I didn't cry.

I didn't speak. I just watched as everything I had ever known slowly disappeared behind a veil of white. And ahead of us–something entirely unknown.

At the airport in Rome, something unexpected happened. We were in the long, slow-moving line for security. I was half-asleep, dazed from the early morning, the weight of the snow, the silence of leaving.

Then, in the line next to ours, I met the eyes of a girl I'd never seen before. Just a glance at first–then a smile, then she lowered her head.

She was elegant in a way that stood out even in that crowded terminal.

Not flashy, but composed, self-assured. Her coat was tailored, and her scarf carefully draped. She carried herself like she belonged somewhere important.

She turned suddenly, and for a moment our eyes met again. I thought she might look away again, pretending not to notice me. But she didn't.

She held her gaze, steady and calm this time, and there was something in it—something unreadable but not indifferent. And I didn't move.

I was afraid any step would break the moment. And then she smiled—not fully, but just enough for me to carry it to the airplane, for the duration of the nine-hour flight.

That smile wasn't an invitation. It wasn't a promise since we didn't get a chance to speak. But it was real.

Just a moment, a look, a silent pause in the noise of departure. After security, I lost sight of her. She disappeared into a different concourse, a different destination, perhaps.

I didn't expect to see her again. But about ten hours later, at Kennedy airport, as we stood in the long line for immigration, I saw her again.

Far ahead–same presence, same stillness in the chaos. She was in the company of a woman, perhaps her mother.

Then, two months later, I settled in Brooklyn, adjusting to the cold streets and the strange new rhythm of American life– I saw her again.

I couldn't believe my eyes; I thought perhaps I was dreaming. Same girl. Same elegance.

That third time, I knew something was different. I felt it–not just recognition, but a pull. Like the turning of a page, I hadn't known was waiting.

My life was about to take a turn, and I didn't even know her name.

I stopped. She noticed. And again, we smiled–this time, not in passing. This time, we spoke.

She was just as composed up close, her voice calm, almost musical. She remembered me from the airport in Rome–and again at JFK.

"We came on a TWA flight," she said. "I was with my mother. We had to come to Brooklyn quickly. It was an emergency."

I nodded. "I was on the Alitalia flight on that day."

"Of course you were," she said with a light laugh.

We stood on the sidewalk like old acquaintances, though we were strangers.

Everything about it felt effortless–like a conversation we had been meant to have all along.

There was no rush, no grand declaration. Just the quiet realization that something had begun.

Her name was Josie. She was from Sicily, the same age as me, and just like me, caught between two worlds.

She told me she had graduated from an art school back home and had come to New York only temporarily, with her mother, because of family reasons.

She spoke with that gentle southern cadence I knew so well, but her Italian was mixed now with bits of English, just like mine was beginning to be.

She smiled easily, and when she laughed, it felt like a door quietly opening.

"No boyfriend back home?" I asked one day, half-teasing.

She shook her head. "Not there, not here. I never met someone I really wanted to be with…until maybe now."

We spent more time together after that–walks through unfamiliar streets that soon began to feel familiar, coffee in little cafes that reminded us of home.

Back when we saw each other the very first time, we were strangers at opposite ends of the airport, and from two different regions of our country.

Four months later, we were discovering the rhythm of each other's lives.

We fell in love gently–no fireworks, no declarations shouted into the sky. Just a growing warmth, a shared understanding between two young Italians far from home, who had met in the most unlikely way.

And just like that, Brooklyn didn't feel so foreign anymore. As weeks passed, Josie became part of my new rhythm in America.

Fate had a huge part in our encounter. God was working overtime on my future.

We shared stories from Italy, about school, about family. With her, I could speak freely. I didn't have to explain who I was. She just understood.

But even as I fell for Josie–honestly, naturally–I carried Laura with me. Although she only lived in the quiet corners of my thoughts. I wrote to her once, and that was it.

Josie never asked about anyone from before. And I never volunteered. But life was moving forward. And I was learning to follow it.

After a while, Josie agreed to date me steadily; "On one condition, though," she said.

"What is it, Josie?" I asked.

I was so surprised when I heard what she had to say.

She took my hands, "Look into my eyes, and listen to me carefully," she said. "It's normal to hug and kiss, but no matter what…never ask me to have sex with you. That, for me, comes after marriage. Do you promise?"

All I could do was smile, appreciate her candor, and say, "I promise, don't worry."

I had found a job in Manhattan, in the fashion industry–a place I knew nothing about at first, but I quickly learned to navigate, to contribute, to belong.

Josie and I fell in love–not the hurried kind, but something deep, steady, real.

But this book is not about Josie and me. I've written that story before in a different book.

Here, it's enough for now to say: *She was the angel I had always dreamed of. Honesty and empathy are her main qualities. She was sent from heaven to guide me, to hold me steady through storms I couldn't yet see. We got married. I built my own business. We have*

We lived the American dream.

But before all that–before success, before stability–there was one more turning point.

Exactly six months after we arrived, my father announced he was going back to Italy.

Nothing had changed in him. Not even New York could shake his restless spirit.

He packed everything, gathered the family, and returned home.

Except for me.

I stayed.

It wasn't an easy decision. I was twenty. But something in me knew this was where I was meant to be. My life was here now. My future had already begun, even if I couldn't see all of it yet.

And so, as they flew east, and I remained. Alone, for a while. But with a quiet certainty that I had chosen my own path, and that it would lead somewhere that was worth following.

Laura was out of my life completely, my heart had been taken by the girl I saw at the airport, on the day I left my country.

Laura made it clear from the beginning, America wasn't for her. She was the only child, tied to her parents, her home, her land.

She had no interest in crossing the ocean. And I understood.

But part of me always believed that when you truly love someone, if that love is deep enough, you follow them.

No matter where life takes you. You go.

She didn't. And so, in time, I let it all go, the memories, the what-if, the silent ache I carried across the Atlantic.

Josie was different. She is different. When her own family decided to return to Italy, she also had to choose.

She chose to stay. All alone in a foreign country, with no certainty, no promise, only love. She believed in us. She stood by me.

And because of that, I gave her everything I could. A life. A family. A future. Not perfect, not without struggles–but built together, with love at the center of all.

We're still together, Josie and I. Fifty-seven years. That kind of love doesn't come twice.

After years of hard work, after building a life in a land that gave me everything–freedom, opportunity, love–I became the one who made the call.

It was no longer my father pulling us back and forth between countries. This time, it was I who reached out to him. Not for his sake alone, but for the future of my five younger siblings.

"Come back," I told him. "There's more for them here than you ever imagined."

And they did. They all returned to America, each of them starting fresh, building their own stories under the same sky that had welcomed me.

All of them came back except my sister Antonietta. She married in Italy and stayed behind, choosing her path just as I had chosen mine.

I missed her, of course. But I understood. We all find home in different places.

Looking back now, I realize: the journey wasn't just mine. It was for all of us. A ripple that started with one decision, one sacrifice, one stubborn hope–and grew into a life bigger than I could have ever imagined.

What comes next in this story is no longer about Laura, or Josie, or even about me.

What comes next belongs to my half-sister Lucia.

Some loves never leave you. They don't burn out or break apart. They transform.

They fold into the soul and stay there, quiet and constant. Like a candle that doesn't flicker, even when the room grows dark.

Lucia was the beginning of something I didn't understand at the time.

When we met, I was still becoming myself, unsure of where I stood in the world, still wearing the clothes of childhood, still speaking the language of obedience and wonder.

And she…she was light. Curious, kind, devout in ways I didn't know how to be.

We were young. Too young, maybe. But what we shared was real. No matter what anyone said then. No matter what became of it.

She chose a different life. A life behind walls and silence and prayers. And I went on into the noise of the world. But she never left me. Not really.

Her name was and still is in every diary. Her voice is in every memory. Her face is somewhere in the corner of every dream I didn't tell anyone about.

Lucia. My sister.

I don't know if she ever knew the full shape of my feelings. I don't know if she ever guessed how much space she still held in my life, even after I had crossed oceans.

As I write, I know exactly where she is. In a better place. A quieter place. She's with God.

Wherever that place may be, I want her to know this:

She mattered.

She changed me.

And that the rest of this writing is for her.

Chapter 21

My whole family eventually returned to America, all except Antonietta. She married and settled in Airola, the same town where Lucia, my half-sister, had spent her life in the convent.

The two of them grew close over the years. Antonietta visited her often, sometimes spending holidays together. She kept me here in America connected to Lucia through letters, stories, and little updates passed around the dinner table like something sacred.

But while the rest of us built new lives, one story remained unfinished; my father's silence toward the daughter he never publicly acknowledged.

Legally, emotionally, publicly–Lucia didn't exist as his child. And in all the years since returning to America, my father never once brought up the idea of recognizing her.

Not once.

I tried. I truly tried. Many times I tried to change his mind. Quiet conversations. Direct appeals. Sometimes gently, sometimes with anger.

"Daddy, she's your daughter," I'd say. "She belongs to us. To our name. Don't you think she deserves at least that?"

But he would brush it off. Change the subject. Say nothing at all. He never had the courage–or perhaps the humility–to face the music.

And so Lucia remained in the shadow of our family's story. Known. Loved, yes. But never officially claimed.

I traveled to Italy often over the years. Business at first, then more for family, and sometimes simply because I missed the land that shaped me.

And every time I returned, I made it a point to visit Lucia. She had grown into a serene, graceful woman. There was something in her presence–still, strong, unshaken by the world–that always humbled me.

She never asked for anything. Never complained. She had accepted her life in the convent not as a burden, but as a calling.

Still, I knew there was pain beneath the surface. A kind of quiet sorrow that never quite left her eyes.

We'd sit in the garden of the convent, or in the small parlor where guests were allowed, and catch up. She wanted to know about my daughters, about America, about Josie.

She had a soft spot for Antonietta, who most of the time came with me when I visited her. But sometimes–when it was just the two of us and the silence lingered–I would ask her the question neither of us could escape.

"Do you ever think about it? About being part of the family?"

Lucia would look at me gently, almost with pity. "Felice," she would say, "I've always known who I am. But your father…he has to carry what he didn't do. Not me."

She forgave him long before he ever asked for forgiveness. And maybe that was what made it harder, his silence was louder than any words could have been.

My parents lived in Brooklyn, growing older in the same neighborhood where we'd first arrived decades earlier. Life had slowed down for them, but the past never seemed to fade–it simply lived quietly between the moments.

Then came the autumn of 1992.

It was the end of November. I was in my office in Manhattan, busy as always, when the phone rang and my mother's voice came through, tight with worry.

My mother's voice trembled over the phone. "Felice," she said. They took your father to the hospital. Something's wrong with his stomach. He's in the emergency room now."

I left everything behind–the phone still off the hook, papers scattered across my desk–and rushed out.

The drive from Manhattan to Brooklyn felt endless. Every red light was an enemy, every second stuck behind traffic was unbearable.

All I could think was, *What if this is it? What if I don't get there on time?*

When I finally arrived at the hospital and pushed through the doors of the emergency room, I saw my mother sitting alone on a plastic chair in the waiting area.

Her purse was clutched tight in her lap, and her eyes were red from crying. When she saw me, she stood up immediately.

"They are running tests," she said. "He's in a lot of pain."

I hugged her, and for a moment she let herself lean on me, like she used to do when I was still a boy. I hadn't seen her look so frightened in years.

"Ma, how long has he been like this?" I asked.

"He had minor problems in the past, for many years. You know how stubborn your father is when it comes to seeing doctors."

"I know, Ma. Perhaps something he ate that didn't agree with his stomach?"

"I don't think so. Anyway, he didn't want to tell anyone," she said. "He thought it was just the usual stomach pain...but last night he couldn't sleep at all. This morning he collapsed."

I sat down beside her, heart pounding, and we waited. Hours passed before the doctors came to speak to us–scans, blood tests, consultations.

Then came the words that changed everything: liver cancer. Aggressive. Advanced. Maybe four to five months.

That night, as we sat at his bedside, and the shock began to settle, my father looked at me with a tiredness that wasn't physical.

That was when our conversation began, the one we never thought we'd have.

The hospital room was quiet, too quiet for what we had just heard. The oncologist had just left, after delivering the kind of news that feels like a blow you can't brace: he explained everything to us, including my father.

"Four to five months left, at most. Maybe less. Sorry," he said, and then left.

My father sat at the edge of the bed, staring at the floor. He wasn't a man easily shaken. He had faced a war, immigrations–but now, his hands rested heavy on his knees, and I could see they trembled slightly.

I sat beside him, unsure how to start. Finally, I said, softly, "Papà, are you okay?"

He didn't answer right away. Then, in a low voice, almost like speaking to himself, he said, "I always thought I had more time…to fix a few things."

I knew exactly what he meant.

"You're talking about things in Italy. Perhaps Lucia?" I asked.

He looked at me, his eyes suddenly wet. It was the first time in my life I saw tears in my father's eyes.

Sobbing he said, "I should have listened to you, and done this long ago. I was a coward, my son."

So when he found out he was dying soon, Lucia was the first thing on his mind. That was a good sign.

I place my hand on his shoulder. "It's never too late, Daddy."

He looked up at me, "How is it possible, she's so far away, and I'm dying," he said.

"Daddy, you're not dying tomorrow, or anytime soon. You'll be out of this hospital in a few days," I said.

"I'll go with you. I'll take you there," I said, squeezing his hand.

He turned to me, as if trying to read if I really believed that, to see if I really meant it.

He tilted his head. "Do you think she would even want to see me? After all these years? After what I did to her?"

I nodded with a smile. "Yes, Daddy. I do believe she would. Not because she needs it–but because you do. You have the chance now, before it's too late, to do something right."

He was quiet again. Then he whispered, "So you'll come with me then?"

"Of course. I already said I would," I added. "We'll go together. You won't have to face it alone. I know it's not easy, but you will die in peace, at least."

"The sooner the better then," he said, "While I still have strength."

He reached for my hand, and in that moment, I saw not the strong, distant man who raised me, but someone deeply human–wounded, afraid, and ready, finally to make peace.

In the days that followed we were curious about how my father contracted liver cancer. He was not a drinker–just a little wine with meals, never more.

But the doctors traced it back to something older, buried deep in his past. As a prisoner of war in Africa during World War II, he had contracted malaria. It had never quite left him, and now it had come back in the cruelest way.

I took him back to see the doctor, for a follow up visit. On our way out, while my father was using the lavatory, I asked him again, "Doctor, do you think my father can travel to Europe and back?"

"Why not, he's still strong. He has at least three to four months," he said.

For the first time in his life, my father faced the weight he had carried for decades.

He didn't want to die with a guilty conscience. And maybe he finally heard the voice I had raised so many times over the years.

"I want to go back," he said to me, while the two of us sat in the car, on our way home from the doctor's office.

I turned slightly. "Go back to where, Daddy?"

"Back to Italy," he responded.

"Daddy, we already know that," I said.

"But you 're confusing me now. So, what are you talking about? You want to go back to Italy to stay, to die there?" I asked.

"No, son, you don't understand. To see her. To tell her I'm sorry, but I want to come back and die here. This is where everyone I love is."

He didn't mention her name, but I knew what he meant. So we planned the trip. I was to go with him.

One last journey back to the old country, for my father. Back to Airola. Back to the daughter he had never claimed–not of hatred, but out of fear, stupid pride, shame, or something even he couldn't name.

This time, he would face her. Face the truth. And ask for the forgiveness he never had the courage to seek before.

Chapter 22

We began making preparations for the painful trip, in February of 1993.

It was still cold in Brooklyn, the air sharp with winter's final breath. My father's health had begun to decline more noticeably–he tired easily, moved slowly, but his resolve had never been stronger.

My mother stood quietly beside him, supportive but nervous. Josie, always my strength, helped organize everything with me–flights, paperwork, arrangements in Italy by talking on the phone with my sister.

This wasn't just a visit. It was a reckoning.

I traveled with the three of them–my father, my mother and Josie. None of us spoke much during the eight hour flight.

We were all lost in our own thoughts, aware that this journey was unlike any other we had taken before.

This wasn't about sightseeing or family reunions. This was about truth. About forgiveness.

Antonietta, who had remained in Italy all those years, was the one who made it possible. She reached out to Lucia and gently explained everything.

That our father was sick. That he wanted to see her. That he wished to speak to her not just as a man, but as a father–finally.

Lucia accepted. She knew I was coming.

We flew out in early February, the four of us: my father, my mother, Josie and I.

It was the first time in many years that we were all traveling together–not for vacation, not for a wedding or a celebration, but for something heavier, something long overdue.

My father hadn't been back to Italy since he returned briefly and then left again. Now, it was about to return not for pleasure, but for reckoning.

At the airport, he was quiet, more than usual. My mother tried to keep his spirit up with light conversation, and Josie sat beside me, gently squeezing my hand when silence lingered too long.

I watched my father as he stared out the window at the tarmac, lost in thoughts. Maybe he was remembering the last time he briefly saw Lucia.

Maybe he was thinking about what he would say to her, or whether she would even look him in the eye.

The flight itself was long but uneventful. Somewhere over the Atlantic, my father leaned over and asked me, softly, "What if she won't forgive me?"

"Daddy, relax. She already has," I said. "She's opening the door. That's all that matters."

When we landed in Rome and got into the car towards Airola, the old familiar landscape began to unfold: umbrella-like pine trees, olive trees, low hills, villages clinging to the slopes. It was all familiar, but distant.

My father didn't say much, but his eyes were wet the first time we saw the sign for Benevento, then again when we passed through Paolisi.

The visit, the meeting with Lucia was to take place at Antonietta's house, in Airola.

Lucia had never left the convent–she remained there her entire life, she was a nun, devoted to faith and service.

But for this special occasion, she was granted permission to leave the grounds. It was a quiet, rare exception.

Antonietta's home, just ten minutes away, offered a warm and private space for what was about to happen.

She, and her husband went above and behind. She wanted this to be something more than an awkward apology or a cold reckoning.

She wanted to create a moment of peace, of grace, of family. She arranged everything like a small catered gathering. Warm food, a beautiful set table, flowers.

It was her way of softening the edges of what might otherwise have been too painful to bear.

We all arrived together from the airport in Rome, by car I had rented. It was around noon.

My father wore his best suit. He walked slowly, leaning on my arm, but his face was calm. Seriously. Ready.

Lucia came an hour later, my sister Antonietta went to the convent to pick her up. My brother-in-law opened the door and Lucia entered dressed in a nun habit, followed by my sister Antonietta.

For a long moment no one spoke. Just tears coming down everyone's face.

Lucia tried to smile, her hands trembling.

She didn't show bitterness. Not anger either. But with a kind of quiet mercy, just by walking in, she made the room feel lighter.

We were all there—my mother, Josie who had never seen her, and I—watching the moment unfold like something sacred.

Licia stepped forward towards my father. He took her hand. His eyes welled up. "I'm sorry," he said simply. "I was wrong. You are my daughter. And I ask you forgiveness—for everything."

Lucia nodded and kneeled. "I forgave you a long time ago," she said. "But I thank you for saying it now."

She stood and they embraced—father and daughter—for the first time in their lives as something whole.

No fanfare. No dramatic words. Just the quiet closing of an old wound. And the rest of the visit unfolded with unexpected peace.

There was no tension anymore, no awkward silence, no dramatic unraveling of the past. Instead, there was warmth.

Conversation flowed easily–memories were shared, old misunderstandings gently passed over. As if the burden my father had carried in silence for nearly fifty years had finally been lifted from his chest.

Lucia was part of the family; she had always been, and now it was official. She sat beside my mother at lunch. She asked Josie about our children.

She and Antonietta fell into their family rhythm–laughing, sharing stories, finishing each other's sentences like sisters alway do.

It was not a perfect reunion. But it was real. And that made it beautiful.

We stayed in Airola for a little over two weeks. In that time, we visited extended family. My grandparents had all passed by then.

We walked the old streets, shared meals with people we hadn't seen in years. But it was clear to all of us: this trip had one true purpose, and it had been fulfilled.

When the time came to return to Brooklyn–ah, that was different. My father stood once more with Lucia, this time at the convent. She prayed for him, gave him blessings.

He kissed her forehead, placed his hand over hers, and whispered, "Ti voglio tanto bene."*

It was the first time I had ever heard him say those words to her, and we all knew it would have been the last.

We drove to the airport early the next morning. As the plane lifted from the runway in Rome, I looked out over the land that

---

* "I love you so much"

had given me everything—my roots, my memories, and now, closure.

For me, that trip was not just about my father making peace with Lucia. It was about a silent and loose thread of my life finally being tied.

I had spent so many years trying to do what he would not. And now, in his final chapter, he had done it—not just for her, but for all of us.

So on the way back, we all felt it: something had shifted. My father wasn't healed, but he was lighter.

The man who had boarded that plane to Italy carrying decades of silence, now carried something else—a kind of peace, hard-earned and humbling.

During the flight back at one point he said to me quietly, "Son, I'm ready now. Not to die…but to be at peace."

Back in New York, winter still lingered. Life picked up again quickly, but the memory of that journey stayed with me—how it closed a chapter that had been opened too long, how four of us made a round trip, but one of us returned transformed.

Two months later my father was gone. But he didn't die with a guilty conscience. He died a father who finally acknowledged all of his children.

Chapter 23

Lucia's life continued quietly within the convent walls. Mine continued in America–work, family, vacations, the steady rhythm of a life built on perseverance and love.

Years passed, and we stayed in touch always through Antonietta, who remained the link between the two words. We had seen Lucia twice since that first emotional visit with my father.

Each time, she was the same–serene, gentle, always welcoming. Her eyes still held the quiet strength, and her smile carried no trace of bitterness, only peace.

She had no one left from the side of her mother's family. All gone, her grandparents who had raised her, her aunt, the nun, was gone as well.

She had just Antonietta there in Airola, and of course the sisters at the convent.

Then, in 2021–twenty-eight years after my father had passed–I received a phone call that stopped me in my tracks.

It came without warning, the kind of call that changes the rhythm of your breathing. A voice from Italy–a familiar one, though aged by time–my sister Antonietta, she told me that Lucia was dying.

Cancer, that it had moved quickly, quiet. She was still in the convent. There was nothing more they could do. If I wanted to see her again, I would have to come soon.

I hung up the phone and sat in silence. Josie found me like that, at the kitchen table, eyes fixed on nothing.

I told her. She didn't ask questions. She just nodded, came over, and put her hand on mine.

"We'll go," she said.

We flew out the next day. Josie handled the details–flights, time off, the tactical things.

I moved through it all like a man caught between two timelines. I was leaving New York, yes–but more than that, I was moving backward, towards something I had tucked deep in my soul for years.

On the plane, Josie sat beside me, quiet and calm. She knew the entire story about Lucia and I. She had always known.

Some stories are too deep not to share, and Josie had never been jealous. She understood that love takes many forms, and the love I felt for my half-sister, had never really disappeared.

We landed in Rome, then rented a car, and started the drive on the Autostrada del Sole. The landscape passed in silence: olive groves, hill town, vineyards.

My heart beat heavier with every mile. When I saw the sign Benevento, I remembered the boy I had once been.

Josie squeezed my hand. "You don't have to explain anything," she said. "I'm here with you."

When we reached my sister Antonietta's house, we didn't waste time, from there she accompanied us to the convent.

The sky was overcast, the gates just as I remembered–simple, iron, dignified. A sister met us at the entrance and led us through the quiet courtyard, past the chapel, down a narrow corridor where the air smelled faintly of incense and old stone.

Lucia was in her room. It was small–more like a cell, truly. Bare walls, a crucifix, a nightstand with a few books, a bible and a rosary. The bed sat under a window where soft light filtered in.

Lucia lay there, frail, thinner than I had ever seen her. But when she turned her head and saw me, her eyes lit up. That sparkle–though dimmed by illness–was unmistakably hers.

She looked at us in a way like she'd been waiting just for that moment. "Felice Josie," she whispered.

I stepped forward quickly and I took her hand. "Lucia," I said, my voice catching. "I'm here."

She tried to smile, but it was mostly in her eyes. "I prayed you would come…I knew you would."

Josie stood quietly at the foot of the bed, her presence full of grace. Lucia looked at her too and said, "You stayed by his side…you must be an angel."

Josie stepped forward, gently placing her hand on Lucia's arm. "We both prayed for you."

Lucia turned her gaze back to me. "Don't be sad. I'm ready. I've made peace…with life…and with Papa' too."

I nodded, holding her hand tighter. "He came. He told you."

"Yes." she said. "And you brought him. That was your gift to me. I know you did it for me."

We sat there for a while, no need for words. Just the silence of love between a brother and sister, one born of difficult beginnings, but made whole through time, truth and forgiveness.

Before we left, she said softly, "Promise me something, Felice."

"Anything, Lucia."

"Keep living with your heart open. Like you always did."

I kissed her forehead. "I promise."

The years, the memories, the family we never fully had–all of it was there in our eyes. She whispered a blessing to Josie.

And then we sat with her, in silence and in prayer, and after a while we left.

While Lucia spent her final days there at the convent, Josie and I stayed with my sister Antonietta, just ten minutes away.

Each morning, Josie and I would rise early, share coffee with Antonietta, and then make our way to the convent.

The short drive felt longer each day–not in distance, but in the weight of what I was carrying. I was walking a thin line between two lives: the one I had built in America, and the one I had left behind.

After our fourth visit, while still in Airola, a sister from the convent called Antonietta in the early morning. "Antonietta, unfortunately I have bad news," she said. "Your sister Lucia passed away during the night. I'm very sorry."

The pain was heavy. The sisters had prepared her with such dignity–she looked peaceful, almost untouched by suffering, as if the last light in her had simply drifted upward.

Josie and I went back to the convent to see her one last time. The chapel was hushed, cloaked in morning light and silence.

A few candles flickered near her simple coffin. Her rosary was wrapped around her folded hands, and beside her was a small bouquet of wildflowers, just like the ones that grew near the path to the river.

Several nuns gathered around us, offering words of comfort. One of them, the same sister who had led us to her room days before, said to me, "She loved you. She always spoke of you with pride."

The funeral was held the next day in the convent chapel. A modest ceremony–quiet reverent.

Antonietta, Josie and I sat together. I didn't say much. I couldn't. I just listened to the hymns and let the memories of her fill me.

Her laughter as a young girl, her faith, her strength. Her grace even in silence.

The burial felt like the closing of a sacred chapter in my life—one filled with unanswered questions, missed years, and finally, reconciliation.

She had lived her whole life in quiet devotion, carrying herself with dignity despite the injustice that shadowed her beginning.

And in the end, she was surrounded by those who truly loved her. Lucia belonged to us, and now, she belongs to eternity.

The morning of Lucia's burial was grey and still. The sky hung low over the hills of Airola, as if even the weather understood the solemnity of the day.

The convent bells rang gently as the sisters led the quiet procession—no fanfare, no elaborate ceremony, just a humble farewell for a woman who had lived with grace without complaint.

Antonietta stood beside me, tears quietly running down her cheeks. Josie held my hand. We followed behind the simple casket carried by a few local men from the parish who had known Lucia all her life in the convent.

She was buried in the small cemetery just behind the convent. A white cross marked the spot, with her religious name and dates carefully carved.

There were flowers from the convent, from neighbors, and from us. I placed a single rose beside the headstone and whispered a prayer I could barely finish.

There was an ache in my heart—not just for the loss, but for everything that might have been. But also, a deep sense of peace.

She had forgiven, loved, and lived with honor. In her quiet way, she had brought our family together, even if only briefly.

She had accepted the pain without resentment, and left behind a legacy of strength and quiet mercy.

On the plane back to America, I kept replaying her last glance, her blessing, the warmth of her frail hand in mine.

Lucia never asked for anything.

But in the end, she received what mattered most: recognition, love, and a rightful place in the hearts of those who had once left her behind.

She was my sister. And now she lives in my memory, in my story, and in my prayers together.

After the burial, we stayed a few more days in Airola. I visited the grave once more before we left. I bent down, pressed my hand against the cool marble, and whispered a final goodbye.

I promised her again what I had said in her room–that I would carry her memory light, not as a burden, but as a blessing. Then Josie and I flew back to New York.

I looked out the window during takeoff, and for a long time, I watched the land fall away beneath the clouds. I knew I might never return to that place again. It was no longer home–it had become a resting place for the people I once loved.

And sometimes, that's where we must leave them, so they can rest, and so we can go on living.

Chapter 24
The Distance That Remains

Since Lucia's passing, I haven't returned to Paolisi or Airola.

Those towns, once the center of my youth, of my awakening, of first loves and hidden truth, have become something else now—cemetary of memories.

My feet have never stepped again in those old familiar streets, but my heart remains tied to them. Every street, every corner, every breeze that moves through those hills carries with it the weight of people I've loved and lost.

My sister Antonietta is still there. We speak from time to time, and she keeps me updated on life back home, but I haven't seen her since Lucia died.

We speak often—by phone, by WhatsApp, even through Facebook. Technology has become our bridge, and through her, I remain connected to that part of my life.

She tells me how things are in town, how the seasons change, who has come and gone.

And every year, on the Day of the Dead—November 2nd—I make sure that flowers are placed on Lucia's tomb. Fresh, simple flowers.

A sign that she is remembered, not just as a nun or a half-sister, but as someone who mattered deeply. Someone who, in her quiet way, shaped the man I became.

Distance does not erase love. Nor does time. And sometimes the most lasting goodbyes are the ones we carry in silence, year after year.

The reason I haven't been back it's not out of anger or neglect–it's the silence that follows deep emotion, the kind that time does not erase, only quiets.

Perhaps it's selfish. Or perhaps it's the only way I know how to protect what's still whole inside me.

After all these years, America became my home. My roots may have started in Paolisi. But my branches grew far away.

And now, with so much behind me, I find myself looking less towards where I came from and more towards what remains here–my wife, my children, my grandchildren, and the stories I carry.

I don't know if I'll ever go back. I suppose some part of me already has–buried there, where so many pieces of my past now rest.

Final chapter—What remains

It's been a few years since Lucia passed, and even more since that winter morning in 1968 when I left everything behind to chase a future across the ocean.

Life gave me so much more than I ever expected. I built a home, a family, a business. I loved, and I was loved in return.

I lived the American dream not just for myself, but for my wife and children, and for the roots I carried from a small town in Italy.

But through all the years, through all the chapters in my life, my half-sister Lucia remained present.

Not in a loud way, but in the quiet spaces: in the sound of church bells on a Sunday morning, in the scent of cypress trees when I returned to Airola, in the silent pull of memory when I opened old letters or looked through family photos.

She had no future, no title, no great fame—but her presence shaped me. Her grace taught me what it means to carry sorrow without letting it darken your soul.

She reminded me that forgiveness is not just a gift you give others—it is one you give yourself. I often think of that final visit, the way she looked at me with peace in her eyes, not blame.

She had every right to hold resentment. But she never did. She understood things we struggle to explain—family, dignity, the meaning of belonging.

I am an old man now. I have seen the world change many times. But I still carry her with me. In memory. In gratitude. And in the silent promise I made to her before she died: that she would not be forgotten.

I often sit quietly now, in the stillness of my home, and think about the journey that brought me here—from the narrow streets of Paolisi to the crowded sidewalks of Manhattan.

From the stone seminary walls to the hum of machines in my cutting factory. From the silent grace of a girl in a theater to the voice of a sister in a convent, whispering my name.

Life moved forward. It always does. It carried me from love to heartbreak, from family ties to family responsibilities, from sacrifice to rewards.

I found my purpose not only through ambition but through the people I loved–the ones who stayed, the ones who left, the ones I lost.

Lucia is gone. So is my father. And my mother. My siblings are scattered between continents and states. I remain, still in touch with the past, but not trapped in it.

Josie is still beside me–my angel, my partner, my constant. Together, we have built a life. Three daughters, now grown, strong and brilliant.

The American dream? Yes, I suppose. But also something deeper: a sense that nothing–none of this–was wasted. That even the pain had meaning. That even the unanswered questions helped build something true.

I haven't returned to Paolisi, Rotondi, or Airola. I don't know if I ever will. But I carry them with me. In the food we cook, in the language I still speak in whispers to myself, in the stories I've written down so they won't disappear.

This book is not for me. It's for my half-sister Lucia, whose life was quiet but worthy. It's for the boy I once was, full of wonder and doubt.

And it's for anyone who's ever carried love across oceans, who's ever left home only to discover it never really leaves you.

Lucia may not have had a father in the way that she deserved, but in the end, she had a brother who loved her–and who will carry her story until the last page is written.

"And this, dear readers, is that final page. In the end, we are all just stories. And this-- this is mine."

Acknowledgments

First and foremost, I thank the quiet hand of Providence that guided my steps from Paolisi to Brooklyn and back again, and that placed the right people beside me at every turn.

To *Josie*, my wife of fifty-seven years–angel, partner, and compass–thank you for choosing the unknown with me, for believing in our dream when it was only a suitcase and a promise, and for turning every house we entered into a home.

To our daughters–*Antonella, Nelly, and Nadia*-who grew into women of courage and compassion: you are the finest pages of my story.

To *Antonietta*, my sister and steadfast bridge between two continents: your letters, calls, and open door in Airola kept our family stitched together across oceans and time.

In loving memory of *Lucia*, my sister and quiet grace, whose forgiveness taught me more than any sermon. This book is, above all, a place for your name to live openly forever.

To my parents, *Domenico* and *Antonietta*–for their sacrifices, their flaws, and the lessons hidden in both. Papa', your final act of courage gave this family its overdue peace.

To *Laura*, whose early kindness helped shape the boy I was becoming; and to my friends and teachers in Paolisi, Benevento, and Brooklyn, who filled my formative years with challenge and possibility.

To the extended *Falzarano* family–on both sides of the Atlantic–thank you for the meals, stories, and laughter that reminded me where I came from.

I am indebted to the medical teams in *Airola*, and *Broolklyn* who cared for *Lucia* and my father with dignity and skill, allowing us the gift of final words.

Lastly, to every immigrant who has ever stood at a harbor or an airport, torn between past and future–this book is an echo of your courage. May these pages offer company on the journey.